"You are always thinking, thinking, thinking."

Étienne's voice was hypnotic. "Never a step taken without calculating the consequences."

Rafi shook his head. "That's not true."

"Isn't it?" He traced a thumb over Rafi's eyebrow, hitching onto his cheekbone before sliding down his face. Étienne's thumb was on Rafi's jaw, his large hand cupping his chin, light enough Rafi could pull away if that was what he wanted.

Étienne lifted his face. "Tell me one time you did something without thinking about it first."

Rafi's breath came out, ragged and broken and barely enough to sustain him. "You know."

Étienne gave Rafi's chin a slight squeeze, like the release of a pent-up tremor. "I want to hear you say it. I want to know that I did not dream it."

Something deep in Rafi sundered, splitting in half those flimsy threads of self-control and duty and fear that he'd believed could hold him together, keep him intact and away from this aching want.

"Say it," Étienne insisted, his fingers firm but still gentle.

"When...when we kissed."

Dear Reader,

Thank you for returning to East Ward and the Navarro family!

Sometimes, there's a trope that a writer loves to write (for me, it's enemies to lovers). Sometimes, two characters jump out at you and demand attention. And if you're very lucky, the trope and the characters show up at the same time.

This is what happened as I was writing *A Delicious Dilemma*, my debut novel. Rafi and Étienne jumped off the page, clamoring for attention. Who was I to say no?

In *The Best Man's Problem*, Rafi is devoted to his family, especially his sister, Val, who helped their father raise him and his younger sister after their mother died. Now that she is getting married to her fiancé, Philip, Rafi will do anything to make her wedding a success. Even if that means helping the best man, Étienne Galois, fulfill his duties, despite sharing a kiss months earlier, after which a panicked Rafi ghosted Étienne.

What starts as a face-off between two opposites turns into grudging respect that blooms into something deeper as both men struggle to cast off their first impressions of each other to see the real person. All while managing to fulfill their responsibilities to the people they care about without losing their hearts in the process.

If you want to know about upcoming projects, sign up for my newsletter or check me out on Twitter, Instagram or Facebook in that order.

Happy reading!

Sera Taíno

The Best Man's Problem

SERA TAÍNO

HARLEQUIN
SPECIAL
EDITION

HARLEQUIN®
SPECIAL
EDITION™

Please recycle

Recycling programs
for this product may
not exist in your area.

ISBN-13: 978-1-335-72454-0

The Best Man's Problem

For questions and comments about the quality of this book,
please contact us at CustomerService@Harlequin.com.

Harlequin Enterprises ULC
22 Adelaide St. West, 41st Floor
Toronto, Ontario M5H 4E3, Canada
www.Harlequin.com

Printed in U.S.A.

Sera Taíno writes Latinx romances exploring love in the context of family and community. She is the 2019–2020 recipient of the Harlequin Romance Includes You Mentorship, resulting in the publication of her debut contemporary romance, *A Delicious Dilemma*. When she's not writing, she can be found teaching her high school literature class, crafting, and wrangling her husband and two children.

Books by Sera Taíno

Harlequin Special Edition

The Navarros

A Delicious Dilemma

Visit the Author Profile page
at Harlequin.com for more titles.

For Charles Griemsman, my mentor and friend.
I will forever be grateful to you.

Thanks to Stephanie Doig
and the entire Harlequin Special Edition team
for your patience and support.

And for my sons.
Art is art and love is love.
You are the place where they intersect.

Chapter One

Rafi

As had become Rafael Navarro's habit over the last several months, he nearly caused another irreversible catastrophe, all because he had butter on his fingers and Étienne Galois on the brain.

Served him right. No one had ordered him to make out with the man, and then ghost him for months. He'd made his bed, and tonight, karma was going to make sure he lay in it.

"¡Ten cuidado!" His father's warning to be careful came as the cake balanced between Rafi and the baker, his friend Simon Santiago, veered at a vertiginous angle.

"Got it, Señor Navarro," Simon said, rescuing the

cake from certain disaster without damaging a single sugar flower.

Rafi was weak with relief. "If we ruin this cake, Val will pin us to the wall with her cooking knives." In fact, if anyone dared ruin Rafi's oldest sister's engagement party to her fiancé, Philip Wagner, they'd have to move out of East Ward altogether. It would be easier than dealing with her when she lost her temper.

"Que dramático," Papi said, smiling indulgently.

Maybe Rafi *was* being a little dramatic, but then again, Papi wasn't going to have the night he was about to have.

Simon wiped their brow. "I haven't stopped for more than five minutes. November is the start of our busiest period, with the holidays just around the corner." Simon's family owned Pan Dulce, the neighborhood bakery where the Navarros—and almost everyone in East Ward—ordered cakes and pastries for every occasion. Cold weather was not a deterrent when it came to celebrating life's most important milestones.

For Rafi, the school year gave shape to his life. Classes were in full swing, and Rafi did what Rafi always did with a precision he'd honed to perfection: Woke at five-thirty to hit the gym before teaching high-school math for exactly 7.45 hours. Graded for another hour before taking the bus home, stopping to check on his father who lived in the same building as Rafi. Relaxed to one of his theoretical-math books or, if he was too brain-fried, watched his favorite show. Helped out at Navarro's on Saturday, the restaurant his father owned with Val, followed by a pickup basketball game with his friends at the community courts. Sunday was his only wild-card day and he usually caught up on schoolwork for the following week.

The methodical routines that ruled his life were indispensable to his well-being. Chaos set his nerves on edge and he avoided disorder at all costs. When systems broke down, things never ended well for anyone. His mother's sudden death had been proof of that. He'd indulged in one bad decision, made one critical change to his day, and now she was gone because of it.

"Time for me to go inside," Papi said, the chafe from standing in the cold highlighting the smooth, olive-tinted brown of his skin, which looked exactly the way Rafi's did when he blushed too hard. Like father, like son. "I'm too old to be out here in the cold, lifting things the size of a Smart car."

"Enrique is a trip. Must be a dad thing," Simon said when Papi had gone inside. "My father might be too old to fix the mixer, but he's never too old to stay up all night playing dominoes."

Rafi smiled, recalling this fact about both of their fathers. He was both blessed and cursed with an almost photographic memory and remembered events with painstaking detail, even the things he would prefer to forget. Especially those things he would prefer to forget.

In Rafi's mind, where every memory occupied its proper place, one recent moment stood alone—a breathtakingly reckless act he'd buried in a dark corner of his consciousness. He'd let go of his iron-cast self-control and allowed himself to have something without a second thought to good sense or consequences. And he'd done it with a person who, according to his own exacting standards, demonstrated the least compatibility with him.

Now, that bone-melting accident of poor decision-making was going to show up tonight. Rafi had done nothing to prepare himself except to fall back on his preferred strategy—pretend it had never happened—and hope Étienne Galois might be relieved enough to avoid the awkwardness and pretend along with him.

They got the megacake—seriously, who needed a cake *that big*?—through the swinging doors leading to the club proper, braving clusters of early arrivals as music streamed through the restaurant and club area. Aguardiente had been closed to the public so Val could throw this party, but the guest list she had supposedly labored over with surgical precision had blown up to include everyone in East Ward, together with what looked like every person Philip had ever known.

"Does she realize everyone she invites to the engagement party is going to expect an invitation to the wedding, too?" Simon asked, reading Rafi's mind.

"I don't know. That's above my pay grade," Rafi gritted out as he pushed the cake past people oblivious to the terror he experienced each time they threw out a limb or forced him to dodge a chair. Rafi's stress level was on maximum overload, from his anxiety about helping Val have the best possible engagement party to the inescapable fact that he was about to pay for one moment of stupid abandon with a long night of awkwardness.

Val waved Rafi and Simon over to a prominently centered table, where the cake would finally come to rest. Her long-sleeved wrap dress matched the sumptuous red color of the hard-sugar hibiscus flowers Simon had fashioned for the cake. Rafi, who had opted for a simple, dark gray cashmere dinner suit over a maroon button-up, approved of his sister's sartorial choice.

"Let's get this up here," Val said, guiding Rafi and Simon as they heaved the sugar monument onto its place of honor.

"I have never been so terrified in my life. I think I aged ten years and I'll never get them back," Rafi complained, dabbing at the sweat that had gathered on his forehead.

"So dramatic," Val huffed.

"Nothing like my sister," Rafi said, finally able to admire the cake without the fear of death hovering over him.

Simon's phone buzzed and they read the notification. "My brother is already texting, asking me where I am."

"Yeah, siblings can be that way," Rafi said, casting a meaningful glance in Val's direction.

"I don't do that," Val protested.

"Girl, what? I have forty text messages from today

alone. 'What are you wearing? The seafood is late. Where are the centerpieces?'"

Val crossed her arms and had the nerve to roll her eyes. "I did not send forty messages."

"Did, too."

Simon's voice cut through the bickering. "Let me get out of here. Don't start dinner without me."

"Wouldn't dream of it. *Gracias*," Val answered, offering her cheek for a parting kiss.

"That cake better taste as good as it looks or I will throw a fit," Rafi said when Simon left.

"Ay, por favor," Val laughed before squeezing his cheeks. "I couldn't have done any of this without you. That's why you're my favorite brother in the world."

"I'm your *only* brother in the world," Rafi retorted. He was Mr. Reliable, the guy his two sisters and widowed father could depend on. With his little sister, Nati, working at the hospital all the time and Val building a life with Philip, it was up to Rafi to keep an eye on him. It's what he'd always done. Help take care of his family.

While Val was in deep conversation with a cousin, Rafi took the opportunity to slip away to the bar, hoping for a drink to unknot his nerves. Rosario Villanueva, owner of Aguardiente, was mixing a drink with a festive flair when she saw him. The music was pumping, and people jostled around him, but the noise was still low enough for him to hold a conversation.

"Hola, bonito, tengo una sorpresa para ti," she cooed.

"A surprise? For me?" He lifted himself onto a barstool and watched as Rosario disappeared beneath the counter. Rafi's curiosity drew him forward to peer at what she was searching for.

She emerged, nearly knocking him in the forehead, the halo of her tight, lavishly styled curls prickling his nose.

"Tan impaciente," she admonished before presenting him with a bottle of Bacardi Facundo Paraíso rum.

Rafi took it from her. "No way, this is so expensive. How did you get it?"

"Your future brother-in-law ordered it exclusively for tonight, among other goodies. You're gonna get wasted on the good stuff." She unscrewed the bottle and poured him a shot. "And anyway, your face says you need it."

"My face does not say I need it. I have a perfectly neutral face."

Rosario set the shot decisively in front of him. "I've known you since you were a little *chaparrito* running between the table legs of the restaurant. You don't have a poker face. Now drink up. It will get rid of all your anxieties."

Where was the lie? Rafi simply didn't possess the capacity to hide his feelings the way his sisters could. He even blushed, which was something his dark skin should have rendered impossible. The idea of seeing Étienne again kept poking at him like a low-intensity but relentless form of torture.

He drained the shot, a premonition creeping across

his shoulders and down his spine. He glanced around, the niggling sensation persisting until his eyes locked on the very person he had desperately hoped he could avoid.

Blood flooded Rafi's skin, a prickling rush like the uncorking of a champagne bottle. He had to look away before his gaze came across as an accusation or, worse, an invitation. Difficult, because Étienne Galois was someone he couldn't ignore.

He was leaning casually on the other end of the horseshoe-shaped bar, demonstrating something on a sophisticated-looking camera to a younger man. Étienne used his hands, his entire body, to communicate, and despite the music and the controlled mayhem of the busy bar, the man he was speaking to didn't look away from him.

Neither could Rafi.

Étienne was a real showstopper, with dark brown skin as flawless as unstriated marble and features that seemed cut from the same, unmarred stone. He'd grown a cropped beard since the last time Rafi had seen him and it made him look both rugged and polished. The delicate blue button-up woven throughout with metallic thread the color of sapphires looked exotic and expensive. A pair of slim-fitting, gray slacks completed the look, the ensemble bringing out the flawless perfection of his skin. The cadence of his words, in Haitian Creole, rolled across the air of the busy club, smoother than the expensive rum he'd been drinking.

At the sound of Étienne's voice, Rafi was back

at his sister's graduation party the previous summer. Rafi had seen Étienne before, but that night was the first time they'd interacted. He remembered the exact moment when Étienne walked into Aguaradiente with Philip, all swagger and confidence, sucking the light and energy from the room and making it his own.

Rafi had had to lean against the bar to catch his breath.

His first thought was that he had never seen anyone so captivating in his life. Étienne was like a spot of color against the dull, gray backdrop of the world.

His second, more persistent thought, was that this man was dangerous. Rafi watched him flirt with everyone, tell boastful stories, throw around his confidence like confetti that clung wherever it landed. For someone as tightly wound as Rafi, Étienne was both exhilarating and terrifying at the same time. Rafi had dated Étienne's type before—all clever jokes and endless bluster, racing from one excitement to the next. The type who didn't fit into Rafi's exacting standards for the men he'd dated. Hell, the last time Rafi had tried, his partner, Roberto, had broken things off because he'd found Rafi too boring. Étienne came off as just another variation on that theme.

And yet Rafi's heart, which had never beat so hard in his life, was choking him with its rhythm.

That night, Étienne had claimed that there wasn't a Caribbean dance invented that he didn't know. Rafi had scoffed at the boast, like everything else that had come out of Étienne's mouth. His stupid, sensuous mouth.

And, of course, his cousin Olivia, who had never met a situation she couldn't exploit for her own amusement, had instigated Étienne to challenge Rafi to a dance-off to prove the point. Laughter erupted as the audience egged them on. Then came the moment when dancing became…something else. The crowd slackened and the hours drained away until somehow, it was only the two of them in a corner on the veranda, and under the influence of a reckless courage, Rafi pulled Étienne down for a kiss.

And because Rafi had known that a kiss was not enough to transform a person, that the Étienne he'd been kissing would be the same Étienne who'd walked into the club, the same kind of blustery, flirty, over-the-top guy who wouldn't want anything more from a bore like Rafi than this kiss, and maybe a quickie if Rafi was lucky, Rafi had forced himself to wake from Étienne's spell, call it a mistake and walk away. A malfunction in his operating system. A 404 error.

The vibration of an incoming text snapped Rafi out of his reverie. He blinked several times before the words on the screen morphed into something legible. It came from the group chat Val set up for tonight, an all-call requesting help. This was her night and Rafi was going to make sure it went as flawlessly as possible. But when he lifted his eyes from his phone, he met Étienne's intense gaze and couldn't tear himself away. The club disappeared and there was only

Rafi, being held in place by Étienne as if he were a
beat away from moving toward him. But Rafi wasn't
ready for a confrontation yet. He broke the brief staring contest, waved at Rosario and slipped away before Étienne thought of coming to talk to him.

Chapter Two

Rafi

Rafi found Val on the veranda. A tender feeling swept through him as he remembered how Val had taken over their household when their mother died. He'd been an eighth grader, she a junior in high school. While the entire family was deep in mourning, and his father desperately so, she'd thrown herself into the role of caretaker, restaurant manager and essentially the glue that held everything together. Val could ask him for anything, and he would give it to her without hesitation.

A set of gold-bangled arms wound around Rafi's neck from behind, the floral scent of Nati's perfume giving his little sister away.

"Hey, *peste*," he said. "Did Val summon you, too?"

"I am not a pest. And, yes, our dear sister has summoned us." She laughed, her voice rising crystalline as a chiming bell against the music playing in the background. Natalía, or Nati, was bright as sunshine, in both appearance and personality. She'd inherited the light-colored curls from their mother's side of the family, and had bronze-tinted skin and pellucid eyes that twinkled with an inner mischievousness. She was only serious when she worked, a sight Rafi wasn't always privy to unless he caught her doing her doctor thing at the hospital.

"You mean, you were allowed to get ready for dinner in peace?"

She sucked her teeth. "Yeah, right. Val had me running errands all afternoon."

"Same."

"Olivia helped me out, though. She's around here somewhere, probably terrorizing the innocent."

"I don't terrorize the innocent." The low words were spoken in Olivia's signature whiskey-and-cigarette voice. "Because there is no such thing as true innocence."

"Baby animals and children everywhere beg to differ," Nati retorted.

Olivia rolled her eyes. "If they mew, bark or whine, I want nothing to do with them."

Rafi gave his cousin a kiss in greeting, which she tolerated. "With that life-affirming message in place, what's the plan? I assume you sensed a disturbance in the Force, as well."

"Summoned before Darth Cupcake herself,"

Olivia chimed in, using Val's childhood nickname in honor of her obsession with *Star Wars* and a disastrous attempt at making cupcakes in her family's restaurant. "Hope it doesn't take too long. Aleysha's waiting for me at the bar." Aleysha, her girlfriend of three years, was sweetly and unremarkably normal, something Olivia could use a little more of.

A warm, accented baritone that Rafi was still inadequately prepared to confront came from behind them. "I am answering the call to service. Olivia, have you hacked anyone into submission lately?"

Rafi's brain buckled under the realization that Val also considered Étienne part of her squad.

"It's been slow, but the month is still young," Olivia smiled, allowing Étienne to leave a kiss near her cheek. Olivia worked as an information-systems security specialist, or, as she described herself, a professional hacker, a job for which her nihilistic tendencies were perfectly suited.

"Étienne!" Nati exclaimed, flinging her arms around him. "You made it."

"It was tricky, *ma petite*, but I managed to reschedule a shoot to be here."

Étienne turned his attention on Rafi. Rafi swallowed, his throat dry as sand.

"Rafael. It's good to see you again."

"Been a few months, yeah?" Rafi hated the uncertainty in his voice.

"Four months and one week, to be precise." Étienne's eyes skimmed over Rafi before sweeping up to hold Rafi's in a steel-forged gaze. No doubt,

Étienne had sized up his outfit, a splurge on his teacher salary, which couldn't compare with the gorgeous blue-shirt-and-slacks ensemble that appeared custom-made for Étienne's long, muscular frame. The way his midnight-dark eyes stared into Rafi's felt like he was stripping him down, peeling away cloth and skin and bone, leaving Rafi exposed, and reminding him of what he'd done.

Four months and three weeks? Wait, was he keeping track?

"Everyone's here!" Val exclaimed breathlessly, with Philip in tow. "Good. Because I can't find the hors d'oeuvres."

Rafi exchanged a look with Nati, the one they shared when Val was about to spiral. "Aren't Papi and Grace handling that?" Rafi asked. "Why are you hunting for hors d'oeuvres?"

"My thoughts exactly," Philip said, sounding more fond than exasperated, which was a relief because Val in control-freak mode could try anyone's nerves.

"Yes, but I don't see them laid out in the kitchen. That has to mean they aren't there. We need to figure out where they are." Val fretted, twisting her fingers together.

"Or maybe—" Rafi took hold of his sister's tense shoulders and squeezed gently "—they aren't there because our father and your future mother-in-law have everything under control. Your job, therefore, is to relax, introduce your respective families to each other and be beautiful."

"But…" Val said.

"But Rafi is right," Philip said, pulling Val in close to his side. He was a full head taller, his blond hair and winter-cream skin glinting in the dim lights of the nightclub. Val fit snugly under his chin. "And while you've got the heartbreakingly beautiful part down—" Olivia gagged under her breath, but Philip wisely ignored her "—you shouldn't be the one worrying. This is our night to be in the spotlight. We'll have more than enough time to stress over wedding planning in the coming months."

"Especially since Darth Cupcake decided to forgo a wedding planner," Olivia interjected.

Nati and Rafi gave each another one of those looks, then shouted in unison, "No wedding planner?"

Nati continued, "With all these people? Why wouldn't you use a wedding planner?"

Val shrugged against Philip's perfectly tailored suit jacket. "I can handle it. It's more work to tell someone what to do than to do it myself."

"You underestimate the expertise of a professional," Étienne said.

"Étienne!" Val squealed, shocking Rafi with her unabashed joy as she pulled him in for a hug. "Did you bring Marielle and Claude?"

"My parents will be here soon. I came ahead to help Alán set up the cameras." Étienne pointed inside the restaurant at the young man he'd been talking to earlier, and he waved back at them.

"Thank you," Val continued. "I feel so much better knowing that you're managing the photography."

"And here I thought you'd only just rolled out of bed," Philip teased.

Étienne grinned at his friend. "Not only just. I've been awake for a few hours."

Philip smiled knowingly. "Let me guess. Premiere? Celebrity birthday?"

"Holiday-edition launch after party. And the after-after party after that." Étienne rubbed the short hairs on his chin. "It was strenuous work."

"Did you even see daylight today?"

"I did when I returned home, and woke as the sun was setting, *Frater*. So I can safely say I saw the sun as it passed me by." Étienne used Philip's college nickname, referring to Philip's stretches of nearly monastic behavior when he'd locked himself away in his dorm room to study for exams.

"As I was saying," Nati interjected, exasperation written on her face, "Val, I can't believe you wouldn't book a wedding planner. It's not like you can't afford it. No offense, Philip."

"None taken. I am, in fact, a regular moneybags."

"Philip," Val said, her voice absurdly fond. Olivia was turning green and even Rafi had to admit, their lovey-doveyness was getting to him.

The rumble of Étienne's voice grounded Rafi. "While I believe Val is perfectly capable of executing a marvelous wedding, there is no need to stress yourself when you can pay others to stress for you."

"I have the best support," Val answered. "Philip's mother offered to help and she's the ultimate party planner."

"Don't forget your best man." Étienne swept a hand over himself.

"Yeah, and I'm the maid of honor," Nati retorted. "Doesn't mean I want to plan my sister's wedding."

"The maid of honor eats and sleeps at the hospital," Olivia interjected. "While our best man here travels fifty out of fifty-two weeks of the year. Are either of you taking time off from your schedules?"

"There is no need," Étienne said, avoiding Nati's pointed are-you-kidding-me? expression.

"Oh, really?" Rafi chimed in, drawing surprised glances because he had been so quiet until now. His anxiety had been steadily climbing until it crackled through him. He couldn't understand how Val, who worried about everything under the sun, wasn't growing anxious, too. "Why is that?"

Étienne scoffed. "Because this is me we are discussing."

"Here we go," Philip said, taking a sip of his whiskey.

Olivia chortled while Nati's eyes grew wide with surprise. Rafi didn't see the humor. Someone like Étienne, careless and overconfident, could ruin a wedding…or anything else. "Does the universe work differently for you?"

"Of course." Étienne side-eyed him before adding, "Everything always works out in the end."

"'Everything always works out in the end,' is not a strategy. It's wishful thinking," Rafi retorted.

Étienne turned his full attention on Rafi, his previously warm eyes growing hard. "I did not imply that I was without a strategy, nor do I start things I cannot finish, as others so often do."

Forget subtext. *That* was a direct hit and it made Rafi want to pull back out of Étienne's striking range. "People miscalculate. Happens all the time."

"Or perhaps people are capricious and inconsiderate." Étienne's eyes flickered with something fierce that he visibly suppressed under a veneer of politeness. "I am not one of those people."

"Rafi's done this before," Nati interjected into the awkward silence that reigned after Étienne's retort. "He was Dariel's best man. Everyone still talks about his bachelor party."

"I heard they had to practically carry everyone out on stretchers," Olivia said. Rafi relaxed, smiling at the memory of Dariel's marriage to his longtime boyfriend, Noah. Dariel was one of Rafi's best friends, an OG member of his high-school-friendship group, which included Simon, their brother, Javier and Caio, Rosario's cousin. It had been an honor to be Dariel's best man. Rafi put together one of the coolest, sports-themed bachelor parties he'd ever been involved in. It was a point of pride for Rafi that he'd been able to give his best friend that experience, something he would have never left to chance.

"That's true." Val nodded, her mind visibly spinning. Rafi sensed her change in mood from the way she chewed on the edge of her manicured nail, her eyes growing unfocused. When she came back to herself, she gave Philip a knowing look. "We've been toying with an idea during the last few days."

This time, it was Philip whose expression grew panicked. "Um, Val, maybe we can bring this up with them later. When we're alone?"

"It's all good, babe," she said, soothing Philip with a caress of his shoulder before turning her attention to Étienne. "We were thinking, since you're so busy with your travel schedule, why doesn't Rafi help you with your duties? You could coordinate with each other and, if something has to get done, Rafi can back you up."

"Va-a-a-al," Rafi said, laughing nervously as he drew out her name. "What are you saying?"

"Yes," Étienne said, his expression revealing the same confusion Rafi was feeling. "Are you suggesting Rafi and I work together?"

"That's exactly what I'm suggesting," she said, smiling with immense self-satisfaction. "Since Nati and Olivia are working closely together, it makes sense for you to have some backup, too."

"Oh, this is gonna be good," Olivia whispered loudly to Nati before taking a sip of her screwdriver. Nati's cheeks grew pink as she bit her lip, looking from Rafi to Val to Étienne as if following a ball game.

Étienne huffed. "Surely, you trust me to be best man on my own."

"Of course, she does," Philip jumped in. "But you yourself said the other day that you'd be on the road a lot. It would make things easier if you had some help."

Étienne turned to Rafi, his expression wary. "What do you think?"

At least Étienne had the decency to ask what Rafi thought, since no one else had. Not Val, who hadn't bothered to pull him aside or send him a warning text—anything to indicate she was about to drop this bomb on him. But, of course, why would she? She'd probably assumed he'd go along with it because he always went along with all her shenanigans. She had no idea what had transpired between him and Étienne, or what it would cost Rafi to collaborate with him.

And Rafi didn't even bother to look at Philip, who was bopping along to her scheme as if it was the most perfect thing he'd ever heard. Philip's support virtually ensured Étienne's participation because the bond between those two was such that they'd do everything in their power to make the other happy.

But it was still a terrible idea. A horrible, terrible idea.

That one forbidden kiss had nearly made Rafi forget every single rule he'd put in place to insulate himself from the spontaneous disorder that could only lead to catastrophe, which Étienne exuded in spades. He couldn't work with Étienne on the most important event of his family's life.

Everyone's eyes were fixed on Rafi, including Étienne's, and he was clearly making his own calculations.

Without warning, Étienne pulled out his cell phone, swiping at the screen.

"Philip, I think your father has arrived."

Philip frowned, glancing at his own device. "I didn't get his message."

"I always said you should change providers," Étienne laughed, pointing at Philip's cell phone.

"I have four out of five bars," Philip insisted.

"Technology, am I right?" Étienne clapped Philip on the back a little too hard if Philip's stumble was any indication. "Says we should meet him at the entrance."

Philip turned to Val. "Will you be okay?"

Val smiled as if they were the only two people in the room. "Of course. I'll hold the fort."

Philip gave her hand a quick squeeze before following Étienne to the front of the restaurant.

As soon as they were out of sight, Rafi took Val by the arm and tugged her to the edge of the veranda, away from Olivia and Nati, who were nattering furiously with each other.

When they were far enough away from his sister and cousin's bionic hearing, he asked in a whisper-shout, *"Que caramba estás pensando?"*

"What do you mean, what am I thinking? I'm thinking of how to make things go smoothly for my wedding—and this seems like a great way for that to happen."

"You should've asked me first."

Val's face fell and guilt crawled through him. "I didn't think you'd mind."

Rafi softened his tone. "I can't work with him. He looks like the type who thinks he's going to wave a magic wand to get his stuff done. And we both know what that means."

"Rafi—"

"It means all the work is going to land on me because he'll be too messy to get it done, and I don't have time for that." This was only part of the truth and he hated misleading her. It's not like Val had gotten him into this predicament. He was the one who'd kissed Étienne, a kiss his sister must never learn about. "I just got the department-chair position. I'm still renovating my apartment, plus you saw him…" Hell, how could anyone not see Étienne? The guy was a walking, talking sex-bomb. Photographer, his ass. Étienne was the guy people took pictures of, not the other way around.

"Rafi—"

"He's so full of himself and I already know he's going to be a monumental pain to work with. He has no clue what the job entails, and I am *not* in the mood to train him. I already have a full-time job."

"Okay, calm do—"

"Don't finish that sentence."

Rafi might not be a paragon of honesty, but neither was he going to allow anyone to treat him as if his concerns were the result of hysteria and not a clear-eyed assessment of his reality. Even if he didn't confess all his reasons, they were still valid.

"Please," Val said, and the simplicity of that one word gutted him. He hated to hear his sister beg anyone, especially him. "Try. For my sake. Étienne's all bluff. He's a great guy once you get to know him and he's actually successful in his own right. He wouldn't be if he didn't have some executive function."

Rafi felt his indignation slowly bleed out of him. "You think?"

"Yes. And who knows?" Her lips curled into a smirk that set off all his alarms. "You might make a meaningful connection with him."

No, not that. Never that. Étienne didn't meet his criteria for a safe, reasonable love interest. They'd connected all right, but only physically and that did not a meaningful connection make.

"That's your angle? Just because two queer guys happen to exist within a stone's throw of each other doesn't mean they'll automatically hook up."

"That's not what I meant."

"Then don't say it. I don't need help getting a guy."

Val placed a hand on his shoulder and squeezed. "I know you don't need help getting a guy. And I know Étienne's a little…exuberant. But he's not the way you say he is. Do you think I would care so much for him if I couldn't count on him? Do you think I'd set you up to work with someone if I thought all he would do is frustrate you?"

"No," Rafi growled, begrudgingly conceding the point. Val would just as soon cut off her own arm as put him in the way of inconvenience.

Val's face softened, and suddenly, she was ruffling the tops of his curls. "Rafi. I'm only ever going to get married once. It's Philip or bust, you know?" She blinked quickly and Rafi held himself very still because he never could handle seeing his sister cry.

"I want things to go well and I know I can count on my family to get it right. Étienne is amazing but he doesn't know me the way you do, and he's constantly traveling. He's also important to Philip. Please, do this for me."

Ugh, this was how his family got him every time. *Familia significa todos unidos.* No matter how much he protested, he was incapable of saying no to either his sisters or his father. They owned Rafi's heart and they knew it.

He let out a low roar of frustration before acquiescing. "Alright. But I'm not responsible for any crimes I'm about to commit."

"I've got your bail right here." Val's face grew so bright, Rafi's heart shifted in his chest, and just like that, he was a goner. If they hadn't been in public, he would have hugged her until she screamed, the way he used to do when they were young. "Thank you. You have no idea what this means to me."

"You owe me. If I ever get married, I want it all back with interest."

"Deal!" She smiled. "I can't wait to be a *titi*."

Rafi pulled back, wrinkling his nose. The chances of Val becoming an aunt by way of him were breathtakingly low, given the current state of his love life. "I never said anything about kids."

"Who are you fooling? You love kids."

"Other people's kids, for an hour at a time, after which I get to send them home when I'm done."

She smacked his shoulder before pulling him in for another hug. *"Tonto,"* she said, and then, *"Gracias."*

When she released him, she gave his hair another unwanted tousle before moving off toward the bride and groom's table, where the wedding party would be seated. Rafi ran both hands through his hair, mourning the loss of time and product he'd used to get every curl to go in the direction he wanted.

"!Caramba!" he swore, trying to pat his hair back into place. He looked up to catch Olivia and Nati observing him.

Olivia chortled, taking a sip of her drink. "This won't be a disaster at all."

"Olivia!" Nati elbowed her, then said, "Rafi, you could've just said no."

"Yeah, okay." A surge of resentment appeared out of nowhere. Nati had been allowed—no, *encouraged*—to find her own path in the world, to strike out and take risks. She was the youngest, the one everyone had rallied around to protect when Mami died. Val had stepped into Mami's shoes while his father dragged himself out of his depressive grief. And Rafi? Rafi had always been stuck in the middle— only boy, middle child, too young to carry the family the way Val had, too old to be doted on the way Nati had been. Rafi had held the center and reached out in every direction he could, whether supporting Nati and her studies, made more complicated by her dyslexia, or helping out in the restaurant. As the only son, it was his duty to be strong and he did his best to fulfill that expectation, to keep at bay the chaos that came with losing their mother, because he was the one who had taken her from them. If he'd have just followed the rules at school and *behaved*...

Rafi snapped himself out of the dangerous train of thought.

He couldn't say no. It wasn't Val's fault he'd briefly let himself fall under Étienne's spell that night, something she never needed to know. He might fuss and complain—he was good at that. But he always gave in and agreed to whatever she asked for. Even if it upended the routines and sense of order he so desperately needed to feel healthy.

"One thing I will say," Nati continued. "With Étienne, you'll never be bored."

"Lucky me." Rafi wanted boring. And calm. He didn't need Mr. Ego on Sexy Legs coming in to disrupt the delicate balance of his existence. He didn't want Étienne exercising his uncanny ability to poke at whatever slept in him that made Rafi want to forget himself.

Chapter Three

Étienne

Étienne followed Philip from the veranda to the bar where he had first seen Rafi earlier in the evening. He recalled his first impression of Rafi at a Navarro family gathering. Rafi had struck him as prickly and rigid, quick with his opinions and even quicker with his disapproval. He'd thought it a pity because Rafi was stunning when he wasn't scowling in displeasure.

But at Nati's graduation party, his initial impression of Rafi changed. Maybe it had been the summer night, clear as polished glass. The sensuous music, excellent food and endlessly flowing Caribbean rum. Perhaps Rafi was under the influence of his younger sister's accomplishment of completing medical school, reveling in it as if it was his own.

Or maybe all these elements conspired to allow Rafi to be who he truly was, a serious man with a razor-sharp sense of humor and an easy laugh that sparkled with joy. Much the way he had been at the bar with Rosario when Rafi had not known Étienne was watching.

Étienne could not resist kissing that version of Rafi.

And then, Rafi had shut him down. He'd ignored Étienne's attempts to communicate. Étienne didn't often experience rejection. Yet, not even his parents' inability to accept his chosen profession had stung the way Rafi's escape had.

Étienne hadn't seen him again…until tonight.

Étienne nearly walked into Philip's back when he stopped at the bar and ordered two whiskeys. "Dad's not here, is he?"

Étienne snorted. "When has your father ever texted me?"

"Valid point," Philip agreed, handing him a drink. It was good. Macallan, from the taste of it. "So why the subterfuge?"

"Your future brother-in-law," Étienne began when Philip had drained his drink, "who, by the way, is quite the character." The music was pumping a soulful Maluma beat that made Étienne ache to move. He loved the music of the islands, had gone out of his way to learn each dance, especially konpa and merengue, which they danced in his country, and salsa for the simple pleasure of it. It was a passion Philip did not share unless his partner was his future wife.

Philip cocked his head at Étienne's comment. "Rafi? He's definitely his own person."

"But is he always so—" *Beautiful? Confounding?* "—contrary?"

"Not contrary, necessarily. Just closed off. Doesn't give up his confidences easily to people he doesn't know." Philip considered his words. "He's only now warming up to me."

"Nothing like Val. She wears her heart for everyone to see."

"She's special." Philip's eyes grew a bit unfocused and Étienne knew he had lost him to some recollection far more pleasant than their current conversation. Philip quickly refocused and continued. "But Rafi has his virtues. He's loyal to his family and committed to his profession."

"Teachers. Ah, yes. The modern martyrs of the world."

The words sounded bitter, even to Étienne's ears. Rafi had a profession Étienne's parents had dreamed of for him. Respectable. Conventional. Utterly unsuited to Étienne's character, regardless of his parents' inability to acknowledge this fact.

"I'm sorry Val sprang the idea of a collaboration on you like that. Are you going to be okay with this? You're not obligated. It was an idea to help you out."

Étienne sighed. This was the same man who, upon meeting Étienne in their freshman year of college, had befriended and guided him through the intri-

cacies of American campus life when Étienne was
newly arrived from Haiti. Philip had done it for no
other reason than because they'd shared a love for
the same soccer team. Philip had charmed Étienne's
parents, bought Étienne's professional photographs
and convinced his own mother to organize Étienne's
first show when no one else was willing to exhibit a
young, untested photographer's work. He could never
deny his best friend anything, even if the sacrifice
in question required him to work with someone as
unpleasant as Rafael Navarro.

"Receiving assistance is not under discussion. It's
the source of the assistance that alarms me," Étienne
concluded.

"Rafi? No, he's great. You'll see. He can come off
as abrasive, but he'll grow on you."

"Pity such good looks are wasted on such an unfortunate personality."

Philip gave him a side-eye that was a little too
knowing for Étienne's taste. "If you say so."

"What do you mean, if I say so? You know my
taste. I like people who are nice to me, who find me
interesting, not annoying."

"You have a lot to say on this subject," Philip said,
pinching a smile back. "If I didn't know better, I'd
say you already ran him through your mental date-
meter and found him...lacking?"

Étienne wasn't having any of this. "Perish the
thought. And anyway, dating him would be like fishing in my bathtub."

Philip's face twisted in confusion. "Fish...what?"

"It's something my mother always says. 'Don't fish too close to home, no matter how tasty the fish is.' Rafi is so close, I might as well be…"

At Philip's grin, Étienne shook his head. "Forget it. The point, is, I would not get near him in that way, even if he wasn't intolerable." That he'd already gotten near him was a point best left unsaid.

"I guess if you did and something happened between you two, you'd have to deal with Val. I'd probably get caught up by association and I'd really like to survive until my honeymoon."

"After a lifetime of living as a monk, we cannot allow that. Even if he were the last fish in the sea."

"In the tub, you mean." Philip's eyes crinkled with mirth. "It'll be interesting to see how you'll work together"

"It will be an act of devotion to you and your bride-to-be. Penance for some hitherto unknown sin." At Philip's burst of laughter, he continued. "Don't judge me, Frater Philipe."

"Not a Frater anymore. I'm officially affianced, and happily so."

"And a far more pleasant person since your deflowering. However, don't expect a wedding gift. Enduring your future brother-in-law will be my gift to you."

"I'll be sure to let Val know not to expect anything from you." The playful gleam in Philip's eyes turned downright wicked. "I could have two best men. It isn't unheard of. In fact, now that I think about it…"

"Don't you dare. I will carry out my duties, even if I am yoked to a gremlin with the face of an angel."

Philip laughed again before his attention was captured by movement at the entrance of the restaurant. "I think your family is here."

Étienne groaned. "The night will be complete."

"Still giving you a hard time about your job?"

He shrugged. "You cannot understand the persistence of Haitian parents. They will be displeased with all my life choices until we no longer share this planet, after which their spirits will take up the accusation."

"That's rough. My father is difficult, too, but it's gotten better ever since I put my foot down. Created boundaries. Maybe you need to do the same."

"That is not how it works in Haitian families. There are no such things as boundaries." Plus, Philip's success was tangible. He had proven himself by softening the edge of his father's fierce management style and taking the company in a new direction. But Étienne's success was of a kind they could not easily quantify. To them, his career lacked security, the one thing they valued above all else. If he wanted their acceptance, he would have to become successful in a way that defied all protests, and it was what he intended to do. "I will fetch them and help them find their seats."

"I'll come with you." Philip set his whiskey tumbler on the counter next to Étienne's and followed him to the entrance.

After his parents were sorted out, Étienne took a moment to relax on the open-air deck, the thick windows facing over the Hudson River now closed against the cold. The Manhattan skyline loomed before him like a mythological creature against the night sky. Étienne couldn't resist the contrast of light and darkness and took out his phone to photograph it, adjusting the saturation and lens speed to compensate for the ambient glare produced by so many competing lights.

He thought about Jacmel, his beloved city in Haiti, before the catastrophic earthquake that struck the island more than a decade earlier. Other memories pushed at the edge of his consciousness—memories of friends, schoolmates and neighbors who were no more. He thought of how one minute they'd been in his life, and the next, they were gone.

But he pressed those memories down beneath the tectonic plates of his mind, the ones intended to keep those terrible experiences at bay. He was not for sadness tonight. He summoned instead the azure of the Caribbean, the frothing coastline that reached toward the white-gold sand and salt-encrusted cliffs, and let them soothe the grief that was always just a memory away.

Étienne glimpsed Rafi from a distance and had to make the supreme effort not to stare at him. The humor of Étienne's conversation with Philip earlier had been a thin veneer for other feelings he was not proud of—rejection, disappointment and a bitterness that oozed like acid if he wasn't careful. No one had ever run from him. It pricked at his sense of self, puncturing his unwavering self-confidence, and he resented Rafi for that.

More infuriating still was the disorientation Étienne experienced every time Rafi appeared. He remembered Nati's graduation party this past summer, remembered Rafi's unexpected humor, his merciless intelligence, the ebb and flow of an energy that grew riper as the night deepened. There was Olivia, daring them to dance, as if there wasn't a Caribbean move invented that Étienne had not learned.

And Rafi, whose pride would not allow himself to be proven inadequate to any task, led Étienne, launching variations and twists Étienne answered with cool perfection, until the point of the challenge had been long left behind.

Hands on Rafi's hips, his fingertips had traced the rhythmic flex of muscle as Rafi swayed to each beat. Every mote of dust disappeared, one after the other, when Étienne discovered the texture of Rafi's dark brown eyes, the flecks of a ligher brown that swallowed the darkness of the corner where they eventually found themselves. Étienne's gaze had slipped down to Rafi's smart mouth, which had gone soft with surrender, lacking all the serrated tartness he usually deployed when he spoke. When Rafi closed the space, all Étienne tasted was an invitation for more, and foolishly infatuated as he was, he had tumbled headlong, gone after what he'd wanted ever since he'd laid eyes on that impossible, beautiful man. He'd kissed Rafi in turn, his awareness of Rafi's body reshaping around the place where their lips met.

Then Rafi had pulled away and told Étienne it

had been a mistake. Left him standing with more questions than answers, because no matter what Rafi said, it hadn't felt like a mistake. That kiss had been one of the most honest, true exchanges Étienne had ever experienced. Impossible to believe Rafi hadn't felt the same electric connection, hadn't sensed the utter inevitability of that moment.

But Rafi hadn't felt what he'd felt, and Étienne had spent all these months struggling with that truth. Despite what his every instinct screamed, Étienne had been wrong. Now, Étienne would have to control his instinctive reaction to Rafi's wide-set eyes, patrician profile and slim, hard build that seemed powered by repressed nervous energy. He had to relegate that kiss to an incident in the past and work very hard to pretend that it didn't matter.

He looked up to see Val at the table reserved for the wedding party, waving him over. Obeying, he was chagrined to find his seat was next to Rafi. They gripped their respective chairs and nodded to each other, after which Rafi did an excellent job of pretending Étienne did not exist, which should not have been surprising to Étienne. After all, it was just a continuation of his behavior of the last few months.

The table filled quickly, including Philip and his mother, Grace, who projected the same unflappability as her son. She gave Étienne something else to concentrate on besides Rafi. Except Rafi had engaged her first, and standing next to him, it would have been too obvious if Étienne had abruptly walked off. He smiled and waited for Rafi to get on with his greeting.

"It's a beautiful party, Mrs. Wagner," Rafi said.

"Thank you, Rafi. Enrique has been a delight to work with." She smiled fondly at Papi, who had been standing on the other side of her. The pride in his father's face was radiant. "We are so very happy for Philip." She blinked rapidly and turned her face away, discreetly dabbing at her eyes.

"We feel the same way. Philip is family." He clapped his future brother-in-law fondly on the shoulder.

Philip held Rafi's gaze, exchanging a quiet understanding with him. It jarred Étienne to see his best friend connect with Rafi in a way that was more than superficial. He did not call it jealousy—Étienne liked to think he was beyond that. But he could not imagine his best friend finding any common ground with that gremlin of a man.

Chapter Four

Étienne

Étienne excused himself to check on Alán and the photographs. Once that was completed, he took his time, moving from group to group with the ease of someone long accustomed to adapting himself to different people, to figuring out ways of not only being tolerated, but welcome. Part nature, part personal training, it was a trick that belonged to those who lived in alien surroundings and had to carve spaces for themselves that were not necessarily promised to them.

Only one person was resistant to all his charms. No matter. Rafi would have to speak to Étienne eventually, if only to get their collaboration under way.

When the first course arrived, Étienne watched

Rafi wait patiently for everyone else to be served before savoring the dish. The small sound of pleasure he made—private, intimate, meant only for himself—sent heat snaking straight to Étienne's groin. The same, unconscious sound of pliant pleasure Rafi made when they'd kissed. A sound he'd never expect the prickly creature sitting beside him to make.

These next six months were going to be torture.

However, no collaboration would take place if one of them didn't break the ice. And it looked like it would have to be Étienne.

"Do you like it?" Étienne asked, indicating the dish Rafi had been sampling.

Rafi froze, pausing in his chewing before swallowing. "It's...delicious actually."

Étienne took a taste of his own serving. "I agree, but the flavor eludes me."

Rafi nodded. "Mofongo in curry and tamarind shrimp sauce." He gave him a sidelong glance, as if he wasn't sure whether to continue or not. "It's an Indian-Caribbean fusion."

Étienne heard the words *curry, tamarind, shrimp* and *fusion*, and barely comprehended them, his attention hijacked by Rafi's profile, one uninterrupted line of perfection from his forehead to his chin. He reminded himself that the face belonged to an unpleasant man who was not interested in him, a man he would have to find a way to work with.

Étienne cleared his throat, returning his attention to his plate, his fork leaving tracks along the craterous surface of the boiled and crushed plantain mound. "I would not have thought to add tamarind to this dish. Am I right to assume Val is responsible for this creation?"

"Kind of," Rafi answered. "The basic mofongo recipe was passed down through my mother's family, but the fusion is Val's inspiration."

Étienne turned to Rafi, struck by how the light from a garden lantern illuminated his hair. "Are you often the victim of your sister's culinary experiments?"

"She hasn't poisoned me yet," Rafi said, returning his attention to his meal. He snuck an occasional glance at Étienne, which Étienne knew because he seemed to catch Rafi each time he looked. Or maybe it was Rafi who kept catching him. Awareness of Rafi invaded him at the molecular level, preventing his attention from settling on anything else with real depth. He should broach the subject of their working together, but it was as if Rafi had erected an invisible barrier that kept him from coming too close. A burst of conversation from the table behind them provided the cover Étienne needed. He leaned in, dropping his voice to a whisper.

"If we are going to work together, at some point we will have to have a real conversation."

Tension radiated from Rafi's rigid posture. He set down his fork and turned toward Étienne, dropping his voice as well and launching a smile that looked more like a grimace. "Are we really doing this here?"

Étienne, who was no stranger to putting a good

face on a wicked game, returned a fake smile of his own. "Doing what here?"

"This." Rafi waved a finger to indicate them both. The music, low and sumptuous, rolled over them, serving as backdrop to the conversations bubbling up around them. Rafi's frozen smile turned his lips thin and pale, nothing like the lush fullness Étienne had tasted that night, a sensation he'd been trying, with frustrating failure, to block from his mind.

A familiar pettiness rose up in Étienne. He wouldn't give this ornery, difficult man the satisfaction of forcing words from Étienne's mouth. If Rafi wanted to cut him off, he'd have to do the work of saying so. "We will be working together. Why would we not discuss our collaboration? Or did you have another conversation in mind?" One that involved Rafi explaining why he'd ghosted on Étienne after he'd been so sure they had shared something meaningful.

Rafi's smile faltered, his nostrils flaring, and Étienne derived immense pleasure from watching him lose control of his pitiful attempt at indifference. Only in that moment did Étienne realize how angry he was, how diminished he felt by Rafi's rejection, and seeing Rafi sweat was more satisfying than any dish that could be placed before him.

A glance at the other guests around the table demonstrated they were unaware of the verbal sparring taking place within reach of their wineglasses, except perhaps for Val, whose smug expression was like salt in an open wound. From her distance, she probably had the mistaken impression they were getting along.

It would have been easier if Rafi had been less irresistible. For even in a fit of pique, with the heat of anger turning his skin to burnished brown tinged with a hint of fiery rose, and his eyes to flashing bits of darkened amber, he was captivating. Étienne wondered if he'd look the same writhing beneath him… or above him…

Maybe this hadn't been Étienne's best idea, after all.

Just as it seemed Rafi was going to unleash a torrent of irritation, he visibly gathered himself together and—with a slight rounding of the shoulders that Étienne found, to his dismay, was rather charming—gave him a tight smile. "Let's reach out to each other after the party. You still have my number?"

Étienne's laugh drew Nati's attention, whose expression mirrored Val's. The nerve of Rafi. "You know full well I have your number," he said through a maniacal grin. "Maybe update your contacts so you recognize it when I call you."

Rafi gave him a matching, saccharine smile. "I recognized it just fine."

"Good."

"Okay."

The clanging of forks against wineglasses cut through the ice that had fallen between Étienne and Rafi, indicating someone was about to speak. Étienne turned away from Rafi's impenetrable face, and wondered how he had ever thought he had found him desirable. How he could have imagined him as anything other than who he was at this moment—a cold, handsome man whose beauty belied a temper that could cut a person to pieces.

Étienne was quick to abandon Rafi after dinner. Guests splintered off into their own orbits, some to drink and talk, others to dance. Étienne checked on his parents and talked to everyone he knew and more than a few people he did not. His mother always said that, given no other option, Étienne could converse with the walls and make them answer back, an assessment he was not inclined to disagree with.

Étienne should have been long gone. He had an early morning flight and had promised himself he would leave as soon as Val cut the engagement cake. It was not his intention to linger beyond that, and absolutely not his intention to be so relentlessly aware of Rafi, as if some invisible thread bound him to that terrible man. Rafi had long been swallowed up by his group of friends. But still, Étienne stayed, keeping Philip and Val company as guests gave their congratulations before going home. As best man, this was fair. No other reason.

"Olivia and I are going to an after party. I rarely get two days off in a row so I'm going to take advantage," Nati said, bouncing out of her chair.

Rafi mussed her hair, earning him a punch in the arm. "Right, because heaven forbid, you'd use it to, I don't know, catch up on some sleep?"

"Bor-ing. How are you and Papi getting home?"

Rafi glanced around. "We came in with Simon but…"

Philip said, "Val and I can give you a lift."

Val smiled tiredly and Étienne, who had over-heard the conversation, knew the soon-to-be new-lyweds would probably appreciate their time alone. Étienne said he would do anything for his friend, and, as best man, this seemed like the time to step up. Even if it meant spending more time with the thorny bush that was Rafael Navarro.

"Don't worry." Étienne clapped his friend on the back. "I can get Rafi and your father home. You two go—do whatever it is you intended to do."

"Collapse, most likely." Philip stifled a long yawn.

"Wild young people," Étienne teased. "Try not to pull a muscle."

Val laughed brightly, momentarily reviving her. "Rafi, you are going to have so much fun working with him. You'll see."

"Yeah, buckets of fun," Rafi murmured.

Val gave Rafi and Étienne a kiss each, followed by a shoulder clap from Philip. "Message us when you both get home."

"Yes, Frater," Étienne said, pulling a grin from Philip.

"You don't need to inconvenience yourself," Rafi said quickly when Val left with Philip. "Papi and I can take a cab."

"You would have your father taking a cab in the middle of the night?" Étienne could not suppress his horror at the idea. He followed his parents' daily ac-tivities with a tracking app on his phone. He wouldn't dream of sending them out with a driver they didn't know at this hour.

"He's not alone." Rafi's voice held an edge Étienne recognized as his temper rising, but he was not intimidated.

"And is not your own safety of any value?" Étienne snapped back.

Rafi opened his mouth to retaliate but his father's firm hand on Rafi's shoulder pulled him back. "*Mijo*, it isn't polite to turn down an act of kindness." He turned to Étienne. "We would be grateful to take up your offer."

"Thank you, sir." Étienne dipped his head in acknowledgement. "I will pull the car around." He bit back the smug smile that threatened to break over his face.

"Not *sir*. Just Enrique."

Rafi's face drained of all color, but when his father glanced at him, seeking his agreement, he smiled the most insincere smile Étienne had ever seen. "Let's go."

Étienne shook his head. *Mezanmi*, how were they going to pull this off if the man couldn't even stomach a car ride with him?

Chapter Five

Rafi

Rafi had done everything to keep Étienne at arm's length, employing his preferred tactic of avoidance to put off the inevitable. Judging from Étienne's sly remarks, rejection was not something he was used to, and while they both might have been content to let that kiss lapse into history, this arrangement would inevitably force things to come to the fore. All Rafi wanted was to have a nice night, celebrate this milestone with his favorite people in the world and not have to deal with something he shouldn't have given in to in the first place.

Of course, his sister had other plans.

The universe could have thrown him a bone. Étienne could have had bad breath, rank body odor, or a heinous personality. But, no. Rafi's luck hadn't even yielded the tiniest scrap. What he got instead was freaking glamorous, gregarious Étienne, dressed like the handsome, debonair, fine-ass man that he was, smelling so delicious, it made Rafi's mouth water. And not a hint of BO anywhere in sight.

To add insult to injury, the man pulled up in a black BMW 3 Series sedan that seemed like he'd just driven off the dealership. Under other circumstances, with someone he hadn't made out with and ditched, Rafi would have made small talk about the car because, like any other normal person who didn't own one, new cars fascinated him. But he let the curiosity go. He had to concentrate on getting through the drive with this man.

Having his father with them should have been a bonus, except his father was an agent of chaos, too. When Rafi offered Papi the front seat on the pretext of good manners, his father had refused, saying he'd be more comfortable in the back. That's how Rafi found himself in the passenger seat, his father's quiet snores filling the car within moments of being underway. Rafi might as well have been alone with Étienne.

"He wore himself out tonight," Étienne whispered, listening to Papi's deep, regular breathing.

Rafi exhaled, accepting the olive branch. "It would have been worse if Grace hadn't cohosted." Philip's mother had brought all her organizational talents to bear on tonight's engagement party.

"The evening worked out." Étienne cast him a

look that seemed to linger a beat longer than was safe for someone who was driving.

Rafi squirmed in his seat. He hated how viscerally aware he was of Étienne—the shape of his knuckles as he gripped the steering wheel, the incline of his body as he drove. And the smell that had Rafi imagining sticks of vanilla dipped in a vial of musk, the biting salt of a rough sea underneath. He couldn't hold anything against Étienne. So far, he was being more than polite. "Anyway, thanks for the ride. I don't have a license, so I use hired cars to get around with him."

"No license?" Étienne's laughter caught Rafi by surprise.

"Did I say something funny?"

Étienne pinched his lips together. "At our age, who doesn't have a license? I was sure they were mandatory in your high schools."

"They're not mandatory," Rafi bit out, "but if you must know, my mother died the year before I was supposed to start driving lessons and it turned into something that didn't make my to-do list." He wanted to add "excuse the hell out of me," but Rafi didn't want to do anything that might wake his father.

Time ticked slowly, painfully by until Étienne spoke. "I was unaware. I apologize."

Rafi shrugged, pulling out his phone to doomscroll his social media, which suited his mood perfectly. At least the time would pass quickly until he could get out of this car and away from Étienne. He was lucky for about three minutes before Étienne started talking again.

"I realize the way Val solicited your help may have been…less than ideal—"

"Understatement of the year."

"Despite certain events—" Étienne drew out the words, perhaps to forestall any further interruptions "—I am grateful for your willingness to help."

Rafi put his phone in his pocket, allowing himself to be mollified. "It would mean a lot to both Val and Philip if we could figure out a way to work together on this."

"I agree," Étienne responded. "Your assistance can only be of benefit. Take tonight, for example." He dropped his voice lower at the snort Papi gave in his sleep. "I must return home and immediately pack for an international flight tomorrow morning."

"You have a flight in the morning you haven't packed for…at all?" Rafi glanced at his watch. It was well past three in the morning.

"I know where my passport and camera equipment are. Those are the most important details." Étienne chuckled but Rafi found nothing funny about it. He was about to commit to working with the man on one of the most important events in his family's life and the best he could come up with to say was *I know where my passport and camera equipment are*?

"I don't know, man, but I wouldn't have left my house without having everything ready to go. I hope that's not going to be your approach to being the best man."

This time when Étienne laughed, there was no humor in it. "I've made a half-dozen international trips in the last year alone. I assure you, it does not require the level of preparation a bachelor party might demand."

"Not my fault if you give off a completely laissez-faire vibe, my dude."

"Or perhaps..." Étienne put the car in gear with a little more force than necessary when they arrived in front of Navarro's. He turned with a look of seriousness Rafi would never have associated with him. "Perhaps you may wish to ask yourself why you need to be such a harsh judge of character with little to no information. My dude."

Oh, no, he didn't.

In the space of a few hours, Rafi's existence had been completely upended without any input from himself whatsoever. He was being forced to collaborate with someone he already knew was going to be a monumental pain in the ass, someone he had an intensely awkward history with. And this same mess maker was accusing him of being judgmental? "I am not passing judgment. I am making an observation. A measurable, verifiable observation. It's called *reality*." Rafi was getting warmed up to let Étienne have another piece—or two—of his mind, when a sound from the back seat reminded him they were not alone.

"*¿Llegamos, mijo?*" Enrique's groggy voice sliced the tension that hung thick in the air.

"*Sí, Papi*, we're here," Rafi answered. Étienne

was already out of his seat and at his father's door, opening it with a flare that bordered on exaggeration.

"Door-to-door service, yes, Enrique?" Étienne quirked an eyebrow at Rafi, all charm and civility.

Petty, too. Nice.

"Thank you." Papi stepped out, a bit unsteady in his grogginess. "He's a good one, isn't he, Rafi?"

Rafi resisted the urge to roll his eyes. "Yeah, Papi. Like winning the lottery."

Étienne's smirk practically shouted victory. He could get stuck in an airport forever, like that one old Tom Hanks movie, for all Rafi wanted to see him again. Rafi forced the words out. "Thanks for the ride."

Étienne gave a curt chin nod, Papi's voice thankfully pulling his attention away. "I'm going to sleep." He stifled a yawn. "Thank you, *mijo*. Rafi can make you coffee before you drive home."

"He has to go, Papi. He's got a flight in a few hours and he hasn't packed yet," Rafi said quickly before Étienne got any funny ideas.

"You *jóvenes*, always leaving everything for the last minute," Papi teased, but there was no sting in it. "Be careful getting home."

"I will, sir." Étienne shook the older man's hand.

Papi walked off, pulling keys from his pocket that jangled in the night air. Rafi followed his father's example and shook Étienne's hand, too. It was large and strong, swallowing Rafi's in a cocoon of surprising warmth. The desire to sink into the sensation was chased away by the fact it was Étienne's hand he was holding.

Rafi pulled away as quickly as he could politely get away with. Étienne squared his shoulders before turning on his heel without another word, then retreated to his idling car and pulled away. In moments, the hum of the restaurant's generators droned in the empty street. Unease surged through Rafi at the way their exchange had gone, and he was horrified when he recognized it as regret. He turned, slipping in through the door his father had propped open. Instead of going downstairs, he took the steps two at a time to his father's apartment, checking in on him and wishing him a good night before heading back down to his place.

Rafi followed the same procedure he always did when he returned home. He removed his shoes, leaving them on the shelf in the entryway designated for that purpose, and slid on his house slippers. He then dropped his keys and emptied his pockets into the glass bowl on top of the credenza, removing anything that should be thrown away and tossing it in a small wastebasket designated for that purpose. Rafi briefly admired his perfect little workflow.

Rafi was never going to get along with Étienne. He was an arrogant, fly-by-the-seat-of-his-pants type, reminding Rafi of all the chaotic boys he'd dated in his life. That Rafi had kissed Étienne only made things worse. Étienne was the sort of person Rafi needed to avoid as if his survival depended on it. He didn't need any more spontaneous, bad decisions messing with the precise balance of his life. But thanks to his sister, he was stuck with all that procrastination and devil-may-care ego wrapped in six feet of distracting hotness.

Chapter Six

Rafi

In the weeks that followed, Rafi worked hard not to give Étienne Galois a second thought. Or a first one, for that matter. He was blessedly absent from any voluntary thoughts, and involuntary ones were chased out—something Rafi had to do often. But Rafi was committed to not giving the man any free real estate in his head. Which was good because the high schoolers he was teaching this semester were taking it out of him.

It was later than usual when he finally called it a day, packing up his student papers and laptop, placing everything in the respective compartments in his bag.

"Still here?" came his bestie's voice from the doorway. Rafi's mood lifted instantly. He grinned at Dariel and held up his messenger bag.

"All packed. And you?"

Dariel held up a history textbook and his classroom keys. "Running out, too."

"Walk with me."

Rafi shut the classroom door behind him, the automatic lock sliding into place—Admin had changed all the doors to auto-lock in response to the endless school shootings. New teachers always locked themselves out of their classrooms and quickly learned to keep the keys practically glued to their bodies.

"Why so late?" Dariel asked.

"Student conference."

"Fun." Dariel shook out his shaggy, dark brown hair, the ends skirting past his collar. He was taller than Rafi by nearly six inches. In fact, nearly everyone Rafi knew was taller than he was, so he was used to peering up at his people to communicate with them. "How's the best-man stuff going?"

Rafi deflated. He had done such a good job of keeping Étienne out of his thoughts and here was Dariel, inadvertently dragging him back again.

"It's going." Rafi proceeded to give him a summary of the events of the engagement party, how he'd been finagled into helping a guy he could barely stand with being the best man. He made sure to leave out the fateful kiss from the summer, as if by not bringing it up, he could erase that it had happened.

"You make Étienne sound like a terror."

"Ugh, the worst. I haven't even heard from him.

Probably thinks he can wait till the last minute to get everything done."

Dariel laughed. "Rafi, being dramatic as always."

"I'm not dramatic! I just don't appreciate how I was dragged into this."

They exited the school and dodged other walkers on their way to the bus stop.

"Talk to Val. I'm sure she'll let you off the hook."

"No, man. It's *Val*. She'd give up a kidney without batting an eye if I needed it. I can't say no to her." Rafi shook his head. "I'm going to have to deal with it."

"If you ever need backup, call me. Noah and I still laugh about our stag party. It was incredible."

They arrived at the bus stop, an icy wind blowing right through Rafi's coat. "Maybe I can do something similar for Philip. He's big into *Star Wars*, so it could be a whole theme."

"You see? Your mind's already at work."

"Not like I can depend on my coplanner."

"It'll work out. Your sister's not going to trust anyone she thinks is a liability. You know how she is."

"Her exact words."

The well-worn bus arrived, unfolding its accordion-like doors. They found seats behind the driver. "We might have left things on an awkward note."

Dariel gazed at him in sympathy. "Is it one of those things where you have to apologize?"

Rafi sighed, debating again on whether to share their mutual history and deciding against it. "I couldn't even tell you where things took a turn. It's like every time he opens his mouth…"

"Visceral," Dariel laughed. "With some people, the reaction is so visceral, you can feel them on your skin. Like goose bumps."

Rafi considered Dariel's words, placing them alongside his experience of Étienne. *Visceral* was the perfect description, his reaction bypassing any conscious decision-making on his part. Étienne's presence triggered something electric in him, like an inverted magnet resisting another magnet of the same charge.

"Hey." Dariel broke Rafi's reverie. "If you can survive teaching freshman algebra, you can survive anything."

Rafi groaned. "Don't get me started on my kids this year. Or my department. It's like everything's coming at me all at once."

Dariel shoulder-bumped him. "All while getting no sleep. Living the dream, man."

"Your optimism is hurting my teeth."

Dariel guffawed, drawing the attention of an older woman who'd been deep into reading her rather large novel. "You're so freaking dramatic."

Rafi stopped by his apartment long enough to leave his bag and change before heading up to Navarro's to check on his father. The dining area, with its walls covered in detailed beach and mountain scenes and decorated in bright greens and yellows, called to mind the sparkling luminescence of a Caribbean day. At this hour, it was empty—Navarro's specialized in breakfast and lunch, so customers in the late afternoon were virtually nonexistent. Papi was at the register, his attention on the people moving outside the window as he counted money in preparation to close out the till.

"¿Necessitas una mano?" Rafi asked.

Papi started and gave Rafi a million-watt smile. Everyone said Rafi looked like his father—same slim build, dark eyes and curly hair, skin that turned brown as a chestnut in summer, and gifted with the same inexhaustible energy. What he didn't have was his father's serenity, the belief that everything was going to work out. His father had navigated a lifetime of extraordinary joy interspersed with bleak tragedy and had managed to come out the other side with his gentle heart intact. Rafi had one monumental tragedy in his past, but he had been directly responsible for causing it.

"I have it under control," Papi said, glancing out the window before zipping up the large bills he'd carefully counted and clipped together to store in the safe. *"¿Como te fue?"*

"Work? Oh, you know. Teenagers." Rafi watched Papi's eyes drift to the window again before he locked the register. *"¿Todo bien?"*

"Sí," Papi answered, taking up the cash bag. "Just a few orders on my mind. I'm going to take this to the office. Will you keep an eye on the front? It's late but you never know."

"Sure." Rafi watched his father as he slipped to the back, passing Val as she came out of the kitchen.

"Rafi!" she said, wiping a spot on her shirt with a rag.

"What are you doing? You're wearing the entire lunch menu."

"You're right." She slapped the rag onto the table. "I don't know why I bother."

Rafi cocked his head in the direction of his father. "Have any idea what's up with Papi?"

"What do you mean?"

"He seems distracted."

The quizzical expression on Val's face gave way to barely restrained glee. "If you watch that door, the reason will appear at any moment."

Rafi leaned against the counter and watched the entrance together with his sister. Within moments, the door of the restaurant opened, an elegant woman Rafi knew well entering the shop. Ilaria Rossi, or Señora Rossi, as everyone referred to the widow who'd lived in East Ward since Rafi could remember. Her granddaughter was a freshman at his school. She hesitated, her auburn hair a splash of color against her tan, belted coat.

Rafi frowned at Val uncomprehendingly, but was forestalled from asking her what the big mystery was when Papi appeared, in response to the front door chime. He approached Señora Rossi and handed her a small bag. She opened it, smiling at the contents before closing it again and thanking him with a kiss on the cheek.

"Did she…?" Rafi whispered.

"Mmm-hmm."

Papi turned to where Rafi and Val were perched and waved at them. "Will you close up?"

"*Sí*, Papi," Val chirped. "We got this."

Papi smiled at Señora Rossi. "Ready?"

She nodded, waving at Val and Rafi, who both wished her a good night.

When the door closed behind them, Rafi let his face reflect all his confusion. "What was that all about?"

Val shrugged a little too nonchalantly for Rafi's taste. "Oh, just Dad, wading into the dating pool. They might've already gone out a couple of times."

Rafi couldn't imagine it. His father? Dating? He had been alone for so long, focusing only on the restaurant, his family and his community, Rafi had created a fixed idea of him and dating was not a part of it. His brain was flailing with this new information.

"I'm happy for him but it feels weird, doesn't it?"

Val quirked her head at him. "Papi has been alone for so long. We're all grown up and looking for our own paths in the world—"

"Speak for yourself," Rafi interjected. His father's dating prospects looked better than his.

"You'll find someone. You're too cute not to." Her face grew serious. "Papi has a right to a little bit of his own happiness, doesn't he?"

"Of course." Rafi frowned at his sister. "Did you have something to do with all this?"

Val gave him a bright smile. "I might have invited Señora Rossi to try my lemon tart and encouraged a little exploration in the area."

Rafi's thoughts flew involuntarily to Étienne, the

collaboration, the precise seating, the serendipity of letting Étienne take him home. "I don't know how I feel about this matchmaking side of you."

Val rolled her eyes. "I'm not matchmaking. I see opportunities and I take them."

"Like me and Étienne?"

"Not my fault you can't see how good he would be for you."

Rafi's stomach did an uncomfortable flip. "Good? For me? I don't think so. He's doesn't fit my dating profile."

"Dating profile? Come on. He's funny, intelligent and has enough personality for at least five people. You know you need some excitement in your life."

"I really don't."

"After that last couple of guys you dated? Yeah, you do."

Val's words wounded him. He didn't want to reveal how much it stung to have someone break up with him because they thought he was too boring.

"Speaking of, have you heard from Étienne since the party?"

Rafi shrugged. "Not once. He's so amazing, he probably has everything under control. He'll call when he needs me."

"He has your number?"

Rafi wanted to snap and say he'd had his number for a good while. But confessing that might lead to other confessions he didn't want to make. "He does. And even if he didn't, he'd figure out a way to talk to me. Maybe while you're plying him with roasted goat."

"Who sounds bitter? Give me your phone."

"Val, no, what are you—"

Before he could stop her, she'd snatched his phone out of his pocket and unlocked the screen.

"Wait, how did you get my PIN?"

Val gave him a withering look. "You're so predictable. You've been using the same prime numbers since high school." She tapped away, thumbs flying.

"Tell me you're not…"

Val ended her text with a flair before handing the phone back to him.

He swiped the screen and read the messages. "Come on! 'Hey, partner, just checking in to see if you needed anything?' And heart-eye emojis? Really?"

Val shrugged, which Rafi hated like an allergy. He wanted to toss the phone into a pot of boiling water. However, before he could implement his plan, it vibrated.

"Oh, for f—"

"No f-bombs."

Rafi swallowed back the string of curses that were building up in his chest. "He's going to think we're friends. Dammit."

She giggled while he read the message. "He wants to meet at his place in Flatbush on Saturday to discuss best-man duties." Rafi gave Val what he hoped was his most intimidating death glare. "Does he realize Flatbush is forty-five minutes away by train?"

"If you're worried about helping out on Saturday, we'll be okay without you." She batted her eyes at him. "You're the best brother in the world."

"I can't with you." Rafi tapped his acceptance into the phone, jabbing his thumbs since he wasn't allowed to take out his frustrations in any other way.

"Give it a chance. For my sake."

"It's not like I have a choice. I already said yes."

She squeezed his cheeks, which he both hated and loved, because the gesture was rich with the nostalgia of his mother doing the same thing to him when he was a cherub-faced child. It filled his heart with warmth but also with sadness and he hated the bittersweet way the memories of his mother visited him. He didn't deserve any of them.

"I just want everyone to have what I've found with Philip."

"Ay. Dios. Mío." Rafi drew out each word. "You've turned into one of *those* people."

Val smacked him on the shoulder before they got to work closing the restaurant.

Chapter Seven

Étienne

Étienne was tempted to run to the nearest window of the photography studio with the expectation of seeing pigs fly.

Rafi texted him? After the way they'd...resolutely *not* hit it off the night of the engagement party? The same man who'd completely blown him off after they'd made that brief connection during the summer? Impossible, given the way Rafi had made it understood how much he disliked Étienne and this entire collaboration. And frankly, Étienne was not eager to engage with the man, either.

Rafi initiating contact meant he was committed to making his sister happy, an impulse Étienne could respect. But this was Rafael Navarro he was talking about, and while the ornery man no doubt possessed tender instincts toward his family, his default, as far as Étienne was concerned, was closer to that of a box of razors, ready to slice whoever reached inside.

"Are you okay?"

Étienne started at the sound of Alán's words, spoken in Creole, and accepted the set of prints his assistant handed him. Alán wore dramatically flared, high-waist black trousers that flowed like a long dress, and a cropped, midriff-baring wool sweater in braided gold and pink thread. It was the worst outfit for such a cold day, but the colors picked up the light of the waning afternoon. The table he worked on glowed with the same fading light, turning the smooth surface into shimmering gold. Étienne scrambled for his camera and snapped several photographs.

"What did I say about doing that?" Alán said, even as he preened for the camera.

Étienne grinned. Alán protested being the subject of photographs even as he came alive for the camera. Étienne often teased him for his false modesty, but Rafi's phone call was firmly on his mind. "Do you remember Rafi? Philip's fiancée's brother?"

"How could I not? You've complained about him every day since the engagement party."

"You exaggerate."

"I do not. You talked about him just this morning."

"Did I? You must be mistaken. I have mentioned him once or twice, at most."

"Daily. Has he kissed you again?"

Étienne pulled a face. "No, but equally distressing—he has experienced a sudden change of personality. Look." He handed the phone to Alán, who read the text exchange.

"'Hey, partner,'" Alán teased, handing the phone back to Étienne. "It looks like capitulation to me. Family pressure?"

"Without question. The man behaves like it's a privilege to endure him."

"I wonder where he might have gotten that impression."

Étienne growled, which provoked Alán's full-body laughter. In his disorientation after the events of the summer, Étienne had confided in Alán, who had talked him through Rafi's rejection, because there was no other way to describe his actions.

Étienne normally had impeccable instincts. He was sure Rafi had felt something that night, experienced the same connection as Étienne had. To have gotten it so wrong still left him unmoored. Hadn't Rafi said as much at the engagement party? *People miscalculate...*

Étienne drummed his fingers against his worktable. His subject was currently with her numerous assistants changing outfits for the next set of photos. An A-list celebrity with an upcoming film, she would be headlining the next issue of *Le Mode*. Étienne's phone chimed with the ringtone dedicated to his family. He pulled it out of his pocket, nearly dropping it. He rarely took calls while on set, but he made a hard exception for his family.

"Deidre," Étienne answered.

A small voice came from the background before she could return the greeting. "Yes, Jo-Jo, it's your *tonton*," Deidre said in English before directing her next comments to Étienne. "Sorry. Jonielle's birthday is coming soon. She wanted me to call to make sure you remembered."

"I set a reminder for the party as soon as I RSVP'd."

"Did you hear that, Jo-Jo? Your *tonton* put you in his cell phone. You are very special."

"The most special girl," Étienne cooed.

A shuffling sound indicated that Jonielle had taken her mother's phone. "Are you taking pictures? Granpè says you like to take pictures and put them in magazines."

"I do. Sometimes I put them on the wall."

Jonielle launched into all the things she wanted pictures of. Étienne gave Alán a helpless look when the latter signaled the time by pointing at his watch-free wrist.

Étienne gently interrupted his niece's recitation. "Do you know who I am taking a picture of today?"

"Who?"

"Diana Portier from the new superhero movie."

"Diana Portier?" She squealed in delight. "She is my favorite actress!"

"Is she? If you are very good, I will ask her to sign a photo for you."

Her scream of excitement blasted all of Étienne's negative feelings away. Deidre came on the line, clearly trying to subdue the overexcited little girl. "Now she will talk of nothing else."

"Manman? Papa?" Étienne switched to Creole.

Deidre sighed. "Stubborn as oxes, those two. Papa overdoes his physical therapy and Manman acts like she can do everything she used to do when she was in her thirties. I had to drag her inside when I caught her scrubbing the steps. No matter what I tell her about building management, she insists on cleaning the stairs."

Étienne couldn't catch his breath, he was laughing so hard at the image of his dainty mother scrubbing away outside of their home. Between his father and his stroke, and his mother with her bad back, there was no peace for his sister.

"If it's any comfort, she never listens to me, either."

"I have missed you. You've been gone too long."

Étienne's mood shifted again, and he was suddenly exhausted. "I don't want to spend every visit discussing my work with Manman and Papa."

"They worry about you. They don't mean anything by it."

"Don't you worry about me?"

"Oh, I know better than to do that." She dropped her voice. "I have all your magazines stored away. One day, they will understand how important your work is."

A surge of emotion choked Étienne's words. "I love you, *boubou*."

"I'm not so little." A bone-curdling shriek arrowed through the phone. "They're fighting over toys again. I must go."

"I have an appointment on Saturday, but I will stop by afterward. You can take off with Paul and have a date night."

"Or a nap would do," she said breathlessly before signing off. Étienne pocketed the phone. His sister's support of his work counter-balanced their parents' dismissal, for which he could not be grateful enough. But it still stung—he wanted nothing more than a version of the pride their parents bestowed on Deidre's profession as a business analyst. Pride he could not seem to earn.

And soon, he would be meeting with Rafi, who was the most dismissive person of all. Not about his work, but about his…character? That someone who barely knew him could be so infuriatingly judgmental boiled his blood, but beneath it, there was another, more vulnerable feeling he couldn't ignore. He wanted the ornery creature to like him. He shouldn't care, since Étienne could barely tolerate him in turn. But the desire to be seen and accepted by him lingered stubbornly.

He squashed the feeling. Rafi wanted to do the right thing by his sister? Good. Étienne would outdo him in fulfilling his obligation and make him regret ever underestimating him.

At the designated time, Étienne paced the top of the train-station steps to keep warm as he waited for Rafi to appear. When Rafi sent his message with the estimated time of arrival, anxiety shrieked like static through Étienne and he had to remind himself he was able to charm some of the most high-maintenance people in the world. He could certainly get along with Rafi for a few hours. After all, Val had suggested this as an assist to him, though he was convinced he didn't need the help. He had to treat it as he would any other assignment that needed to be done. Liking the person he was asked to work with was not a professional requirement.

When Rafi's head appeared at the top of the stairs, Étienne closed the app he'd been scrolling and shoved the phone into his jeans pocket. Rafi's brown eyes locked on his and Étienne was momentarily stupefied. The forest-green scarf tucked into a snug, black pea coat brought out the olive-brown undertones of his skin. Étienne's heart clanged loudly in his ears and he shook off the feeling, reminding himself that this was work, and therefore nothing to get excited about.

Étienne stepped forward, ready to take Rafi's messenger bag from him in a burst of courtesy, when Rafi tripped and went down. The passage of time became a crawl as the toe of Rafi's boot caught the top step, unable to clear it in time. Étienne rushed to close the distance, hoping to catch him or blunt his fall. But his reflexes had been befuddled by Rafi's arrival, and he'd been too slow to come alive. Rafi's right knee bore the brunt of impact with the concrete, while his messenger bag cushioned his hands from injury.

"Are you okay?" Étienne asked, kneeling beside Rafi, but Rafi waved him away.

"Great," Rafi growled, pushing himself gracelessly to his feet and wincing when he put weight on the right leg. "Just great."

"I'm quite serious," Étienne insisted, especially when Rafi winced again. "Maybe you should see a doctor."

"Don't know anyone in my network out here in Flatbush. One of the perks of being on the school board's insurance plan." He grimaced as he opened the flap of his messenger bag. "At least my laptop is in one piece. So—" he slung the strap across his shoulder with finality "—where are we headed?"

Étienne surveyed him again, unconvinced that he was fine. He gave a quick nod in the direction of his apartment. "Left at the corner."

Rafi swept his hand out with exaggerated courtesy. "Lead the way."

Étienne assessed Rafi as his walk devolved into a pronounced limp despite efforts to mask the fact. Rafi's bottom lip was pinched between his teeth, so it was obvious he was in pain. But the man was proud—Étienne had gathered that right away—and would surely not admit to it. Something about this blunted the edge of Étienne's anxiety. He wouldn't call it pity; even the thought felt like an offense toward Rafi, but an acknowledgement that in Rafi's place, Étienne would have been endlessly mortified.

Étienne looked for something to distract Rafi as he struggled with his injury, and considered the neighborhood he lived in, the community that had embraced his family when theirs was ripped apart.

"That is Nanette's Grocery. It's where my mother buys all her spices."

Rafi blinked rapidly, as if waking from a daze. "What?"

Étienne panicked a bit but pushed on. "I was pointing out the grocery. My mother says Nanette's has only the best and she can't be bothered trying anyone else."

He groaned inwardly at Rafi's impassive face. Why was Étienne still talking?

Ever so slowly, as if surrendering to an impulse he didn't trust, Rafi's pinched expression softened into a hint of a smile, and Étienne had to concentrate on where he put his feet before he ended up on the ground, too.

"Sounds like my father," Rafi answered. "He's been shopping in the same grocery store since he came from PR, even though there's a Sam's Club a few blocks away."

Étienne brought his gaze back to him. "With them, it's not always about saving money, is it?"

"No." Rafi's face became impassive again, as if having a civilized conversation with Étienne was a violation of some rule he'd set for himself.

When Étienne stopped at his brownstone, so did Rafi.

"This you?" Rafi asked.

"Yes." Étienne calculated the number of steps and the mechanics required for Rafi to get himself upstairs with his bruised knee. But lingering too long was out of the question, as well. He took the stairs slowly, pretending to be engrossed in the hedges beneath the first-floor windows in the eventuality that Rafi might need help. But Rafi limped without complaint, grimacing each time he put weight on his injured leg. He was a stoic. Or simply bullheaded.

In Rafi's case, probably both.

"I'm on the third floor," Étienne said when they entered the hallway.

Rafi's face fell, possibly at the thought of navigating all those steps. But he swallowed and put his hand on the banister. "Let's go."

"No." Étienne's mind scrambled for a solution before settling on the obvious and least-desired option. He directed a murderous glance toward the back of the hallway, dredging words up through the stab of panic that threatened to shut down his lungs. "There is an old service elevator in the back."

He was sure Rafi would protest and insist there was nothing wrong with him or his leg, and he would take the stairs, thank you very much. Instead, he visibly exhaled.

"I'll follow you."

Étienne had somehow hoped Rafi would turn down his offer, but the poor man had no other choice, unless he wanted to crawl up the stairs. Spasms rippled through Étienne as they drew closer to the wicked contraption, but he held his reaction under tight control, watching the metal door that hid darkness and the promise of terrible memories within. He almost turned away except Rafi's injury gave him no other choice.

The elevator was a small, rickety thing Étienne refused to use, as he did most elevators except when they could not be avoided. They triggered all his anxieties about constrained places devoid of light. Devoid of escape. Reminding him of that night years ago when Jacmel had been shaken to the core of the earth itself, until it had crumbled under the weight of bone and rubble around him. *On him.* His heart raced and sweat beaded across his forehead. With Rafi·mere inches beside him, the elevator grew as tiny as a matchbox.

"Been a long time since I came out to Flatbush. At least a couple of years." Rafi voice pierced the fog of Étienne's mounting terror.

"For the cultural festival?" Étienne tried not to pant as he spoke.

"Yeah. I've only come a handful of times. It's a hike from my house."

"I…" Étienne grimaced, closing his eyes to head off the vertigo before opening them again. Were they only on the second floor? "I didn't… I'm sorry. I'm so used to driving I didn't give inviting you over a second thought."

"People my age should have licenses and cars, right?" Étienne grimaced but Rafi shrugged. "It's whatever, man. The ride was a straight commute. Well, except for the Midtown switch, but I didn't wait too long. You okay? You don't look good."

"A bit warm, is it not?" The explanation could pass as truth. Sweat trickled down his sideburns, threading through his short beard.

Rafi stared at him, his brow furrowed. "It's forty-five degrees outside and there is a draft blowing up through the elevator shaft."

Étienne exhaled. "I'm not fond of elevators."

"Claustrophobia?"

Étienne nodded, taking a shaky breath.

Rafi reached out to place a hand on Étienne's shoulder. It might have been his imagination, but the wild crescendo of Étienne's pounding heart relented somewhat at his touch. Rafi's frown disappeared, giving way to an expression Étienne could only describe as *soft*. "I'm sorry. If I had known, I would have insisted on the stairs."

"With that knee?" Étienne said around a pant. "Nonsense." The door slid open on Étienne's last word. "See, we're here already. No harm done."

Rafi's frown returned but he said nothing further. His hand slid away when Étienne escaped on the pretense of holding the sliding door in place for Rafi to step through. Étienne's breathing was slowly returning to normal and the achy tension at the center of his chest was dissipating. Now, all he wanted was a nap.

"To be sincere, I didn't expect any communication from you after the engagement party."

Rafi paused in his limping to answer Étienne. "Val caught me off-guard when she suggested we collaborate, and I might have been impossible to deal with as a result. I don't handle sudden changes too well." Rafi stared up at him, his gaze direct and unflinching. "I owe you an apology for the way I acted at Aguardiente."

"I was perhaps not at my best, either." How could he, with all that lurked in the background of their interactions?

"Just wanted you to know."

Étienne nodded solemnly, knowing this was not the only conversation they needed to have, but it would do for now. "Let's go inside."

Chapter Eight

Étienne

Étienne unlocked the door and switched on the lights. He watched Rafi take in the oriental runner that split the corridor in half like a hot dog, the living room visible from where they stood. Following Étienne's lead, Rafi undid his coat and jacket, then removed his boots, though it cost him some effort with his leg. Étienne slid a pair of guest slippers toward him, Burberry print lined with wool. Rafi's voice was conversational despite a certain breathlessness that was no doubt the result of his knee.

"Once Val gets an idea in her head, it's hard to get it out," Rafi said.

"A family trait, perhaps?"

"Fair enough. But I want things to work out for her,

so here I am. Besides——" Rafi shook his head as if describing a toddler "——she snatched my phone when I told her we hadn't texted each other."

Of course, Rafi would not have initiated communication with Étienne on his own. Why had he hoped it would be otherwise? "I will fetch ice for your knee."

"Don't bother. I'm fine."

"So you have repeated numerous times. There is a chair and an ottoman in the living room. It might ease your leg if you sat there."

Rafi scowled, but limped over to the indicated seat, sinking with slow, obvious relief, and pulled his leg onto the ottoman by the material of his pants.

"Would you like a drink?"

"No, I'm good."

Apparently, *no* was Rafi's favorite word.

Étienne sighed. Here was Rafi, young, beautiful and abused by this misadventure, and an unexpected pang of sympathy for this contrary man snaked through Étienne. He'd been dragged against his will into a collaboration with someone he clearly did not want to be around, powered by guilt and obligation, unwavering in his commitment. And damn Étienne's instincts. He couldn't help but want to ride in and save this man from himself. Because this, he realized, was Rafi trying. And Étienne owed it to Philip and Val to try, as well.

"Be back."

Étienne expected another protest, but Rafi closed his eyes and leaned back against the sofa seat, giving Étienne a thumbs-up. Étienne quickly assessed Rafi.

He was shorter than Étienne, a fact made more obvious by the way the leather sofa seemed to engulf him.
He was wiry, but not rail-thin, his muscles prominently outlined by the green sweater that matched
his scarf. He had substance, but not bulk. As tension
slowly drained from Rafi, the lines of his face grew
smooth and his scowl melted away, and Étienne was
back in Aguardiente, watching him laugh, watching
his face break into an expression he had only ever
directed at Étienne the night they kissed.

Étienne escaped to the kitchen, making quick
work of bagging the ice, and returned, bypassing
Rafi and his ready *no's* to place the pack gently on
his knee. Rafi's eyes flew open and he held Étienne's,
his expression unreadable. Étienne froze, waiting.

"Did I hurt you?" Étienne asked.

Rafi studied him for a few beats longer, the seconds ticking by to the thunderous rhythm that pum-
meled the inside of Étienne's chest. "No. It feels
good. Thanks."

The air grew heavy with something sharper than
Rafi's acquiescence. Every word seemed balanced
on a blade's edge, as if the wrong one would slice
them both to ribbons.

Fetching the water became the most important
thing Étienne had ever done, giving him time to get
his head back in order. He fell into the old habits of
his childhood home, where a glass of anything offered to a guest was served on a linen napkin and
arranged on a tray. Sliced lemons and two tablets
of ibuprofen completed the offering. He returned to

the living room, where Rafi was rummaging in his computer bag. Despite his earlier rejection, Rafi took the glass and sipped water while Étienne placed the tray on the end table next to Rafi. Rafi's dark brown eyes tracked his every move.

"Fancy." Rafi swallowed the pills before setting the glass down, its bottom clicking against the silver.

"It would have been inconceivable in my parents' home to hand something directly to a guest. Old habits die hard."

Rafi nodded, his eyes discreetly taking Étienne in from top to bottom. But his expression remained shuttered and Étienne was as lost as ever to understand what he was thinking.

"I was checking out your decorations." Rafi pointed at the artifacts that adorned Étienne's apartment. "Are they all from Haiti?"

"Some come from the different countries I've visited. But most are from my island. I like to surround myself with reminders of home."

"A little like your mother insisting on shopping at Nanette's."

Étienne smiled despite himself. Rafi had been listening. "Something like that." Rafi's computer was open on his lap. "And you? Are you like your father?"

Rafi briefly narrowed his eyes before pressing the power button, the computer's CPU whirring to life. "Depends who you ask. Most people say I'm exactly like him."

"And what do you say?"

Rafi took a deep breath. "I'll never be as good as

he is." He pointed at a framed picture prominently displayed over a writing desk. "Who are they?"

Étienne smiled at the picture of Xavier flanked by their schoolmates, as if he could smile back from whatever worlds he roamed. Xavier's bright eyes and open expression frozen in time as the witty, daring teenager who had been Étienne's first friend, first kiss, first everything. "It's a special photograph." Most of the pictures Étienne had owned of his friends back home had been lost in the earthquake, except for a handful he'd been able to recover, all framed or tucked away in his diary. "My best friend in Haiti."

"Does he still live there?"

Étienne's smile faltered. Even after more than a decade, he could not say the thing. He couldn't quantify the terror of the night, the people who did not escape because the earth had crushed them, grinding them until they were nothing but broken bodies buried in stone. The absence of Xavier and his other friends was a jagged, heart-sized wound beneath his ribs. He glanced toward Rafi, whose lips had parted slightly, the only sign that betrayed his understanding.

"Didn't mean to pry." Rafi dropped his eyes to whatever had appeared on his screen.

"Tell me what you have there." Étienne ignored the rawness of his own voice.

Rafi's gaze remained fixed on his screen. "I, um… I pulled up the file that I used to keep track of all the tasks I completed while I was best man for my…" Rafi's voice faltered but he pushed through. "My best friend."

Étienne noted the pause but said nothing, taking the seat next to Rafi, who turned the computer so Étienne could also see. It was a spreadsheet, all neat columns and color-coded boxes. He got a whiff of Rafi's cologne, sharp and direct, not unlike its wearer, but with an undertone of something delicate, like caramelized sugar. Only a few dulcimer notes, nothing more, but it was enough to entice Étienne into inhaling deeply. Given the heaviness of their conversation, it soothed him, unknitting the gnarl of sadness and nostalgia that had twisted his stomach. He cast around for something to pull him away from the darkness.

"I see you avail yourself of the devil's program," Étienne teased.

"You mean this?" Rafi's brow furrowed, indicating the screen. "You sound like my friend Simon. What is it with people and spreadsheets?"

"They are incomprehensible, and I find myself wanting to leap up and scream at the possibility of grappling with them."

Rafi pulled a face but only said, "I could set up something easier for you to understand. A table in a plain document should do it." He clicked on an icon to launch the word-processing program.

Of course, Rafi would assume Étienne's distaste was a result of him not knowing how to use the infernal program.

"I don't need you to simplify anything," he snapped.

The expression that darkened Rafi's face forced Étienne to take a cleansing breath and calm down before he said something he couldn't take back. "I will learn to appreciate it." Étienne picked up his phone and swiped open the project-management app he preferred. "Why don't you explain how you've organized everything?"

Rafi side-eyed the phone. "It really depends on what Philip wants you to do."

Étienne nodded, the silence stretching for several beats until Étienne came to the realization that Rafi was waiting for some kind of response to his statement.

"We will be meeting this week." This was not entirely a lie. Étienne and Philip met regularly, he just might not have scheduled anything specific for wedding planning yet.

"Right," Rafi said, his expression going dark again as he fixed his eyes on the screen, closing the document he'd opened and maximizing the spreadsheet to fill the browser window. "I guess we can extrapolate a few things so my trip here isn't a complete waste."

An unpleasant prickle of heat erupted on Étienne's skin. He'd simply thought it would be a good idea to play this all by ear until he got his footing. "It isn't entirely a waste, though, is it? You were able to…" Étienne cast around for something to complete that sentence but came up empty.

"Fall on my face?" Rafi growled. Étienne didn't have to know him that well to understand that he was angry.

Étienne swallowed hard. "Show me anyway. I'm sure it will be beneficial."

A muscle in Rafi's jaw worked overtime before he launched into an explanation of the organization of his spreadsheet, as if Étienne had never opened a computer before. Étienne didn't need that level of detail but he had very little space to complain given his own lack of preparation. Étienne chose to endure the entry-level explanation, focusing sometimes on the boxes before him, sometimes on the smooth skin of Rafi's jaw, the hint of stubble that shadowed his chin, the sweep of bone as it melted into the soft spot below the ear. Rafi was good at explaining things without being intentionally condescending, but he was also lovely to look at and it blunted the edge of the Computer 101 explanation he was giving Étienne.

"Then you click the little floppy-disc icon at the upper left corner of the screen, which will save the spreadsheet for you. Just remember in which folder you saved it." Rafi lowered the screen and closed his eyes, perhaps resting them for a moment before turning them on Étienne, who was tapping questions to ask Philip in his notetaking app.

"Are you seriously texting?" Rafi snapped.

"I will have you know—" Étienne turned his screen around "—that I am taking notes. Not texting."

"Whatever," Rafi said, shoving his computer into his computer bag.

"Not whatever." The fragile threads of Étienne's patience, worn thin by the useless explanations Rafi chose to inflict on him, evaporated, and he grasped at the familiar comfort of anger and indignation to forestall the guilt of being unprepared. "I know how to use your devil program. I choose to ignore it because I prefer to use other tools."

"Then why did you make me explain everything?" Rafi demanded, his voice rising at the end.

"I was trying to be polite."

"There's nothing polite about wasting people's time," Rafi complained as he gathered his things together.

Étienne was back to taking deep breaths to calm down. Rafi was simply determined to misconstrue every action Étienne took for the worst. "It wasn't a waste of time. I got a lot out of it. It's just not my preferred method of organization. You have your way, and I have mine."

"That isn't the point." Rafi slowed his frenetic packing and fixed him with a mordant gaze. "I'm sensitive about time because I don't have a lot of it. As for the spreadsheet, choose whatever you need to help you stay organized. I don't care. Just don't waste my time."

Étienne wasn't sure if he preferred indignant Rafi or resigned Rafi. He answered, hoping to mollify him. "I will adapt. Share a duplicate of this one so we can collaborate. I don't mind using it as our point of organization."

Rafi rolled his eyes. "You think you can manage?"

Étienne was close to punching something. "Are you under the impression that I'm incapable?"

Rafi's eyes grew hard, a flush that was not altogether unattractive spreading over his neck and cheeks. "Not incapable, exactly."

"You figure I don't care." Étienne stood, shoving his phone in his pocket with unnecessary force.

Some thread in Rafi also snapped and he wobbled to his feet. "What do you expect me to think? You make me come all the way out here and you've barely done the minimum to prepare. I'm basically giving out a free course on spreadsheets that you don't need and you don't even bother to stop me. What are you playing at? You think my time isn't worth something?"

Étienne squared his shoulders, jabbing his index finger in his direction. "I am not debasing your time. I didn't speak to Philip because I was traveling and believed that with the benefit of your experience, I would be able to have a more informed conversation with him."

"That's just ass-backwards," Rafi said, slinging his computer bag over his shoulder and across his chest.

"Simply because my way of doing things is different from yours doesn't mean it is inferior."

"No, but you're doing things your way at my expense and I don't appreciate that." Rafi limped carefully to the entryway, where he'd hung his jacket and left his boots.

Étienne deflated at his words, and the reminder of his injury. Dammit, this wasn't the way things were supposed to go.

"Wait," he said, reaching Rafi in a few long strides, placing a hand on his elbow. Rafi froze, his dark eyes darting to where Étienne's fingers lightly held him.

"What?" he spat.

Étienne ignored the tone. He'd certainly earned it. "I'm—I'm sorry. You're right. I have not been respectful of your time. I was..." Étienne released Rafi's elbow when it was clear the man wasn't going to run away. "I wasn't thinking. None of this has turned out as I expected. I should have spoken to Philip first. I see that now."

Rafi's face was still dark and moody, but the deep furrow of displeasure between his eyebrows had relaxed somewhat and he didn't look like he was going to lob his computer at Étienne's head. "Okay."

Étienne stepped closer to him, his temper cooled by his outburst. "Don't misunderstand me. If this collaboration is too difficult, I can help you get out of it." He took another deep breath—it seemed breathing was an endless chore whenever he was around Rafi. "But I hope you won't do that. I hope that we can find a way to make this work, for Philip and Val's sake, but also—" he spread his hands in despair "—I have no clue what I am doing."

"So you thought you were going to bluster your way through this?" Rafi said.

Étienne shrugged. "I'd like to think of it as absorbing what I need as I need it."

Rafi chewed his lip thoughtfully before he spoke. "Can we agree that osmosis might not be the best approach here?"

"I thought carrying the ring and planning the bachelor party was the extent of it, but from what I see here—" Étienne pointed to Rafi's computer

"—you are right. Osmosis might not be the best approach."

Rafi chewed on his lip. "I don't want to be that person, but—"

"Oh, go ahead. Say it."

Rafi quirked one corner of his lips. It wasn't a smile but it was the closest thing to one that Rafi had directed toward him. "Since you're trying to be cool about everything, I won't tell you 'I told you so.'"

"How kind of you," Étienne said, not masking the sarcasm. "Though you can be a tad judgmental, Raphael Navarro."

Rafi crossed his arms. "You were the one acting like you were depending on the luck of the universe and your good looks to make things happen. My sister's wedding is important and can't be left to chance."

Étienne gave him his first smile of the day as well. "My good looks, eh?"

Rafi's eyes widened and another blush crawled over his skin before he looked away, fixing his eyes on some indistinct place on the wall. "I mean, you're not ugly."

"I agree. And if I might add, neither are you."

Rafi's narrowed eyes flicked toward him before flitting away again. "Uh, thanks." He cracked his neck and continued. "I'm going to need your travel schedule so we can come up with a timeline and divide up these tasks."

"No doubt there are tasks we can undertake together." Étienne noted the subject change but played along, looking at the notes on his phone without seeing them. He had to crush the surge of pleasure at Rafi's acknowledgement that Étienne was good-looking. It was not the first time he'd been told this, but the comment hit differently when Rafi said it.

"We can start with deciding on the wedding gift, and move on to planning the bachelor party, which is the biggest item on this list. You'll also have to clarify with Philip things like the ring and transportation to their honeymoon. I'll talk to Val about the tuxedos." He tapped his upper lip with his finger, the wheels of his mind quickly turning. "Your idea about sharing this spreadsheet was a good one. I'll do it as soon as I get home."

"I had a good idea? Finally." Étienne's stomach chose that moment to rumble to life. The sound made Rafi's eyes widen in surprise.

"What's living in your stomach?"

"My desire for griot. There is a small restaurant right up the street that makes it." Étienne glanced at Rafi's knee. "I can pick some up for us."

"Thanks, but if you don't mind, I think I'll be heading home now." Rafi put on his coat, scarf and gloves, moving stiffly but without wincing as before.

"You're not too hurt?" Étienne asked as Rafi carefully put his boots on. "I can give you a ride back to East Ward."

"No." There was that word again. "The ibuprofen and ice really helped. My leg feels better. I think it'll be okay."

Étienne closed his eyes, attempting to maintain control over the flurry of contradicting things this man made him feel. Impatience, elation and exasperation, in every iteration. "You got injured making an ill-advised journey on my part. A ride is the least I can offer."

"You can come out to me next time."

Rafi anticipated meeting up again. Progress. "Deal. I'll walk you out, but I do require one more indulgence."

Rafi straightened, his face a mask once more, and Étienne decided he hated it when Rafi closed himself off. "I'm listening."

"You must take the elevator, of that there is no question. But you will forgive me if I meet you on the first floor." He paused, then continued, "An unfortunate consequence of being buried under the rubble of your home for several hours after a catastrophic earthquake."

Rafi stared at him for a moment, the struggle clear. But that stony expression fled, and in its place was something like empathy. "I'm sorry," he said quietly. He limped closer to place a hand on Étienne's shoulder. Without the distraction of his panic attack, Étienne was able to concentrate on the heat and weight of it radiating through his clothes to singe his skin. "You wouldn't have had to relive that trauma if it weren't for my leg."

"It's nothing. You didn't know."

"Now I do and I promise to be mindful of it."

Étienne dipped his head in acknowledgement. He could handle acerbic, judgmental Rafi. But suddenly sweet Rafi, full of understanding and compassion, provoked too many feelings like the ones he'd experienced in Aguardiente. Feelings that, given how things had gone between them since then, would find no outlet.

Étienne opened the door of the apartment, prompting Rafi to drop his hand and follow, his limp much less pronounced than before. "You weren't put out by my…moment in the elevator?"

"Me?" Rafi chuckled softly. Étienne locked the door and they moved to the back of the hallway. "You'd be surprised at what I run into in my line of work."

Étienne paused in front of the elevator. That's right. Rafi was a teacher. "Trauma has no respect for age."

"You'd think the younger you are, the easier it would be to recover from things, but it's not true. Those wounds just end up rewiring a person."

Étienne knew he was thinking of his mother. It was one of the first things he understood when getting to know Val—the total void their mother's absence had created in the Navarro family. Étienne could complain about many things, but he still had his Manman and Papa and his sister. They'd all survived that terrible night and the migration that took place afterward, and he was thankful every day for this fact.

He didn't realize how long the silence between them had stretched until the swoosh of the opening elevator doors filled it. Étienne didn't want to ruin this cease-fire with the weight of ghosts and loss, always hovering on the edge of everything.

"I'll probably be off this contraption and out the door before you make it down so, uh, thanks again." Rafi offered Étienne his hand. It wasn't true—the elevator was horrifyingly slow and Étienne's long legs would make flying down the stairs the work of a moment, but Rafi was ready to go and he did not want to strain the progress they had made.

Étienne took Rafi's hand, squeezing it firmly, but gently. It was a nice, strong hand, a bit rough in places. It had character, a story to tell, not unlike the person who owned it.

"Send a message when you arrive," Étienne said, releasing his hand.

Rafi nodded before turning away to step inside the metal jaws of that infernal machine.

Chapter Nine

Rafi

Rafi's leg felt better upon leaving Étienne's apartment, but that feeling wore off quickly. The train ride home left Rafi breathless with exhaustion.

His emotional state was a little more complicated.

He had gone all the way to Étienne's house, expecting to be annoyed. Étienne accomplished that by being woefully unprepared, therefore wasting his time. As a bonus, Rafi had brought back a wrecked leg for his troubles.

Even with all that, it hadn't been terrible at the end. They'd managed to muddle their way toward a plan. Étienne wasn't quite the chaos demon Rafi envisioned, though the proof would be in the results.

It didn't help Rafi's state of mind that Étienne

had looked good enough to eat in a stretched-to-the-last-thread sweater and snug jeans that hugged every single last curve and angle, making Rafi lose his equilibrium and smash into the pavement like a Looney Tunes cartoon.

Payback, he supposed, for ghosting the man.

Rafi's throbbing leg sent pain permeating through his every thought by the time he limped back to his building.

Rafi couldn't afford to take time off from work, especially not this week. In addition to his normal workload, he was launching his after-school tutoring program and leading a training. He needed to have this knee looked at to assess his options.

When he finally stumbled through the door of his building, he considered walking up to Nati's apartment to see if she was home, but his leg rebelled against the idea of taking any more stairs. Instead, he shot her a text, hoping she'd have a minute to reassure him that his leg wasn't going to fall off.

"If it was broken, you'd be in a lot more pain," Nati said in her no-nonsense, work voice when she called him back from the hospital.

"Trust me, it hurts like hell."

"But you're still walking. Tell Val to bring you in."

"Are you kidding me? She'll freak out."

"Fine, grab a cab. I'm getting off soon, but I'll wait and get you looked at by the doctor on shift."

"You already worked all day. I got this."

Nati clucked her tongue. "Whatever, I'm heading to radiology to let them know you're coming. See you in ten."

She ended the call before he could protest any further. Val might be the queen of the Epic Spiral, but Nati was the Unmovable Force. And Rafi?

Dramatic?

Judgmental?

Mr. Dependable on a good day?

God, he had to be able to do better than that. Étienne, with his maniacal energy and his power of *yes* had a much better rap going on than he did. Gorgeous. Huge personality. Exciting. Had he mentioned gorgeous already? Even if he was an unmitigated mess, he was more interesting than anything Rafi had going on. It wasn't fair that one person should contain so many perfect multitudes.

When Rafi arrived at the hospital check-in, Nati was already leaning against a wheelchair, waiting for him. Rafi shuddered at the pristine white walls, the reflection of the tile floors and the smell of antiseptic and metal that sunk like daggers into his lungs. His mother's death had ruined hospitals for him. While Nati had turned her trauma into something good, Rafi avoided all reminders of what he'd done.

"You don't need to be here. I told you…"

"Right, like you'd leave me if the roles were reversed. Now stop being difficult." She tapped the wheelchair. "Hop in."

"I'm not sitting there. I can walk."

"Don't care," Nati said coolly. "Sit. I'll take you back."

He was about to continue his objections when a doctor in a white smock like Nati's arrived, cutting off Rafi's protest. She was a tall, white woman with a heart-shaped face and bold, arched eyebrows that looked like someone had painted them onto her peaches-and-cream skin. She was definitely a nine-out-of-ten in Rafi's book and, because he knew his sister, it was clear by the way she was doing everything to not look at her that she thought she was a nine-out-of-ten, too.

"Dr. Navarro. Is this your brother?"

"Yes," she answered, a little stiffly. "I thought Dr. Reinhardt was on rotation tonight."

"We traded shifts." Her eyes lingered on Nati a moment longer before she redirected her attention to Rafi. "I'm Dr. Young, the physician on duty. I'll take you back to Radiology."

Dr. Young waited for him to sit. Rafi sighed. He wasn't going to escape taking a ride in the wheelchair tonight. He figured he could make an issue out of it, but he didn't want to make a scene at his sister's job, especially with the weird vibe Nati and Dr. Young were giving off. It was his turn to tune into his little sister's drama, instead of the other way around. He sank into the chair, accepting his fate.

The conversation between Nati and the other doctor was stiff and full of medical jargon Rafi couldn't get his head around. But the tension was palpable between them and Rafi would never let the chance to rib Nati pass. When the doctor left to speak to the radiology tech, Rafi turned to his sister.

"Nice lady."

Nati sniffed. "She's alright. Kind of a pain in my ass sometimes."

"That's the pot—"

Nati thwacked his arm. "I'm not a pain."

"You are too a pain. Come on, tell me. You look like you woke up naked next to her without knowing how and now you have regrets."

Nati's eyes flashed with something that Rafi took as a victory. He could barely contain himself. "Why are my sisters so scandalous?"

"*Callate.* Weren't you supposed to see Étienne today?"

"Yes…" Rafi hedged because Nati's gossip meter was on red alert.

"So? How did it go?"

Rafi groaned internally. Either he was going to have to lie to her, which he was terrible at doing on his feet, or tell her what happened and suck it up, hoping she wouldn't tease him too hard. It had nothing to do with him wanting to talk about Étienne with her. Not at all.

"I…might have fallen down when I got out of the train station."

"That had to hurt. Did Étienne notice how bad you were limping? I hope he gave you a ride home."

"Well…" He proceeded to fill her in on the general details of his visit, how he fell on his face right in front of Étienne and insisted on coming home afterward on his own power. He filtered out some of the information, things that belonged only to Étienne. Like the grocery. His claustrophobia. The picture of his friend.

"You fell on your face in front of him? Way to make an impression."

"Not my best moment."

Nati elbowed him. "Did you have fun otherwise?"

"It wasn't torture."

Nati peered at him, as if trying to figure something out. "You spent the entire afternoon with Étienne and all you have is 'It wasn't torture?' I'm not buying it."

"What do you want me to say? That I swooned at the sight of him, after which he rescued and carried me off to his lair to seduce me with ibuprofen and ice before delivering me back to the world of the living in his BMW?"

"That was oddly specific."

"I promise, it was all work. Hard labor. *Trabajo.*"

Nati rolled her eyes just as a tech arrived to collect Rafi and set him up for the X-ray.

After, they were banished to a waiting room until Dr. Young returned, holding Rafi's chart. "Good news. No evidence of fracture. Lots of rest, ice for your knee and anti-inflammatories for the swelling. I'm also prescribing a compression bandage to help support your leg until the bruising goes down." Dr. Young accepted Rafi's thanks, then dipped her head toward Nati, a gesture his sister returned before Dr. Young left to tend to her other patients.

"You sure you don't have more history with her?" Rafi asked as Nati insisted on wheeling him right out to the exit.

"A momentary lapse. Nothing more." Nati's face grew unreadable.

"You're lying."

"Am not."

"Are, too. You guys are all up in my business with Étienne, a situation which, I might add, I was dragged kicking and—"

"Are you seriously trying to pull the victim card?" Nati exclaimed.

"Yes, I am very much pulling the victim card. I don't appreciate the situation I am in."

Nati laughed out loud. "You are so dramatic! May I remind you that I was the one who said you didn't have to agree to this whole situation? You don't get to turn things around so you can look like a victim after you made a conscious choice that you could have avoided by simply doing what I told you."

"Well, I'm not the one who got into a hit-and-run with Doc Sexy." Rafi leaned in. "She was doing some serious pining back there. Is that how you leave all the boys and girls?"

"Oh, sure" she exclaimed. "Let's talk about my hookup to deflect from the fact that *A*, you are too much of a pushover for your own good, and *B*, you actually had fun with Étienne and you're too extra to say so."

"Hookup! You admit it!" Rafi nearly shouted as the car she ordered arrived.

"Deflecting again," she said, helping Rafi a little too roughly inside the car, then taking the seat next to him. "You had fun. Admit it."

Rafi loved the taste of victory but he would not be slandered. "There was no *fun* involved with working with Étienne. It was a total waste of time." Rafi whisper-shouted so the driver wouldn't hear them.

"No me vengas con esas tonterías."

"It's not foolishness."

"Who knew you were so short on self-awareness. Oh, wait, I did."

"Not with the short jokes."

Despite the bickering, when they arrived at their building, Nati helped Rafi down to the basement and eased him onto the sofa, where he stretched himself out in relief. She packed him a bag of ice, tossing it from the kitchen, and he barely caught it.

"Your bedside manner needs work," Rafi grumbled.

"My bad," she deadpanned. "I'll pick up the compression bandage."

"You love me."

Nati glared at him. "There's no crime in changing your mind. Just because you weren't happy about working with Étienne doesn't mean you can't decide he's not bad after all."

"You trying to set us up, too?"

Nati pulled a face that was comically exasperated. "I am not the sister who is so full of romantic optimism that she would try to shove someone you don't like in your face. But your options don't have to be that extreme. It's not love versus hate. You might also consider that you have a chance to make a friend."

"That sounds…uncharacteristically mature. Who are you and what have you done with my sister?"

"Ay, whatever. Let me go to the pharmacy before it closes."

"That's right. Better do what the doctor says."

"I'm ignoring you." She opened his door, tossing over her shoulder, "Hibernate or something. I'll be back."

"What did I tell you about threatening me?"

Nati's fist appeared behind the closing front door, and she flicked her middle finger at him before shutting the door completely.

Rafi chuckled, sinking into his sofa pillows. Nati could be annoying, and sometimes, he was a little jealous of how comfortable she was with putting herself in situations where she couldn't predict the outcome. But he was grateful to her because she was the reason he became a teacher. After their mother died, it became his job to take care of his younger sister while Val and their father kept the restaurant going. He helped her with homework and read to her when her dyslexia made studying hard, something their mother used to do. He discovered he liked showing people how to do things. He thrived on the energy of a classroom. He didn't even mind the endless freaking grading. He'd always been into math and science but might not have discovered his joy for education if it hadn't been for Nati.

His phone vibrated and Rafi nearly rolled off the sofa, digging into his pants for it, which would have been brilliant if he ended up trashing his other knee, as well. But those thoughts shook loose when he saw the name on his display. He could've slapped himself. How had he forgotten to let Étienne know he'd made it home? It had been hours since he was supposed to message him.

Dammit. "I'm sorry. I realized I forgot to text you."

Étienne's tone was light but there was an edge to his words. "Good to know you're still alive."

"I'm sorry. I got caught up in the ER—"

"The emergency room? For your leg?" Étienne let out a string of what sounded like invectives in Creole, none of which Rafi recognized and all of which sounded incredibly inappropriate.

"You're the one who said I should have my leg checked out."

"At a doctor's office. Under the assumption that your injury was not severe. I can't believe I let you talk me into allowing you to return home on your own."

Why Rafi's skin was pebbling over with goose bumps, he wasn't sure. "It's not a big deal. I didn't want to go back to school only to discover I'd caused serious damage."

Étienne huffed at his words. "Journeying halfway across New York and New Jersey, I would be surprised if you didn't damage it." His voice grew gentle and Rafi snuggled deeper into his pillows. "Is your knee okay?"

"I lucked out. Doctor says it's just bruised."

"And what was the doctor's prescription?"

"Rest, when I can. Compression bandage. Ice. Anti-inflammatory meds."

"Not so different from my advice. I believe I can safely say 'I told you so.'"

"You didn't give me any advice. You told me to see a doctor and then dropped a bag of ice on my knee."

Étienne's intake of breath was heavy with indignation. "I did not drop a bag of ice on your knee. I placed it there gently. And the comfort of my ottoman? What about that?"

"Yeah, okay, maybe that, too."

"Medicine?"

"What do you want? A medal? Fine, yes. You were a Good Samaritan. Congratulations. I'll make sure to bring you a cookie for your troubles next time we meet."

"Cheesecake, please. I hate cookies." Étienne's laughter came as a surprise, and without wanting to, a chuckle escaped Rafi, as well. He didn't want to laugh, not even a little, but Étienne's was infectious.

"You will be impressed to know I have begun to pack my bags for my upcoming trip, much against my natural inclination."

"And what was that like? Did you burst into flames? Get eaten by the tiny monsters that live in your bag which disappear only when your plane is about to take off?"

"That was quite the imagery. I did not believe you capable of such an elaborate imagination."

"Right, because a math guy can't have an imagination. Stereotyping much?"

"No, I was not making a generalization about math people. Only about you."

"I'm not offended at all."

The silence that followed Étienne's airy laughter wasn't uncomfortable. Rafi's lids grew heavy, and he swallowed a yawn. "I'll ask Val about the tuxedos. You think you can talk to Philip before we meet again?"

"Of course. I won't make the same mistake twice. Don't forget to share the spreadsheet."

"How can I, given your obvious eagerness to use it?"

"I have not stopped fantasizing about it even for a moment." Étienne paused, leaving Rafi waiting in the unexpected space of his hesitation. "We will speak soon, yes?"

"Yes." Rafi didn't make commitments he couldn't keep. "After your trip. I'll be eager to hear what Philip says. It will shape your...our schedule."

"Very good. Well then..."

"Well, then," he breathed. "Good night, Étienne."

"Bon nwi," he answered, then ended the call.

Rafi let the phone fall on his chest, replaying the sound of Étienne's *bon nwi* over and over in his head. It wasn't remarkable—how many times did Spanish fall out of Rafi's mouth during the day? It rarely happened in professional settings, or in places requiring any formality. Only when he was comfortable, at ease. The way he felt now.

And it struck him as interesting if Étienne might also be at ease.

Or it might be his default. Maybe the very definition of Étienne Galois meant he was easy in his own skin, the opposite of Rafi, who fretted and worried about everything all the time. Maybe, *bon nwi* had nothing to do with Rafi and was a manifestation of a serene mind, something Rafi wouldn't have the first clue about. The hospital had reminded him of the terrible consequences of changing things, causing the unexpected to occur.

Rafi's eyes burned with exhaustion. He weighed falling asleep on the sofa against dragging himself through his closing-day routine. He concluded that he had no choice but to hobble to his shower and get ready for bed. But for now, he was content to let his thoughts meander as his eyes fluttered closed, each one landing one way or another on Étienne Galois.

Chapter Ten

Étienne

Étienne emerged through the customs gate after his flight from Jacmel to LaGuardia a few weeks later when his phone lit up with a message from Rafi, almost to the minute Étienne said he'd be back in town.

Étienne considered the message as he stepped out of the way of moving passengers. He was tired after the usual rigmarole of being stopped and questioned by Immigration before clearing Customs, his throat parched from breathing dry, recycled air, which no amount of first-class comforts could mitigate. Full of uncertainty toward Rafi, it was an uncomfortable place for him to be. The ground he'd gained from their mutual reset had, with the passage of these last

weeks, regressed into anxiety, as if they'd never ne-
gotiated a cease-fire.

He swiped the screen.

Val chose the tuxedos. Managed to talk her out of
orange-and-green cummerbunds.

Étienne leaned against one of the columns in the
airport terminal. He didn't know Rafi well, but this
manner of jumping into things *in media res* without
so much as a greeting seemed consistent with someone as goal-oriented as Rafi.

An attachment came through, which Étienne
quickly opened. The photo revealed a headless model
wearing a classic black tuxedo against a white background. His large fingers flew over the keypad.

I am also relieved we won't be dressed as an Easter
choral ensemble.

In Val's defense, Nati was responsible for the terrible colors. Val was humoring her. Maid of honor
and all that.

And you who humor no one at all have saved us
from certain fashion catastrophe.

Étienne tugged his carry-on through the glass
doors leading to passenger pickup. At the taxi stand,
a line of cars advanced slowly toward each baggage-
laden traveler. Despite the jaunty holiday music and

Christmas decorations in the airport, the weather was cold and windy, nothing but a dreary cloak of gray compared to the glinting gold of the island he'd left behind. After an interval of silence, his phone vibrated again.

Are you still out of town?

Étienne tapped out a response. OMW home from the airport. On an impulse, Étienne attached a photo of Jacmel's bay that he'd taken when his hired car had wound up the hill overlooking the water, high enough to capture a view of ocean blue unspooling toward the horizon.

The answer was instantaneous.

You call that work?

An arduous shoot, yes.

I don't care what you were doing, that is not a place you go to work.

The breath Étienne released was a cross between humor and disbelief. Rafi sounded like his parents. *Work is work, no matter the scenery.* Or the purpose. The Jacmel shoot was part of a new photo series he was working on, a departure from the award-winning photographs he'd created two years earlier. Deeply personal, it had been more than arduous. It had been emotionally obliterating, but Rafi couldn't have known this.

A cab arrived and Étienne helped stow his luggage before giving the driver his address. He settled into the worn black leather of the back seat, the tears and balding patches adding to the general grayness of the afternoon. He sent a second photo of the beach for good measure.

Show-off, Rafi texted, quickly followed by: But it's beautiful.

Do you still doubt I was working?

No. Now I'm just bitter.

Étienne leaned forward, elbows on his knees, and tapped away. Jacmel is the jewel of the Haitian coast. Nothing can compare.

Is that where you're from?

Étienne tilted his head, surprised at Rafi's curiosity, though he'd asked questions about his background when he'd come to his flat. Yes. I was born and raised there until we moved to the US.

The response was slow again and Étienne figured Rafi had gotten busy. He leaned against the headrest, closing his eyes for a few seconds of quiet when his phone vibrated again.

That means you were older when you moved here. Eighteen or nineteen?

Étienne stared at the screen before answering. Yes. Eighteen exactly.

A string of dots appeared, then disappeared, happening several times in a row until he replied. That was the same age my father was when he came to the US for the first time. Then, another brief pause before... I always thought he was brave for doing that.

The smile that snaked across Étienne's face came from a soft place. Rafi admired his father, something Étienne could identify with. Your father was brave for sure.

I meant to say so were you.

Étienne stared at the screen, the words losing all shape and meaning. If he didn't know better, he could have sworn Rafi had given him a compliment.

Heart pounding, Étienne could only trust himself to say Thank you. To his relief, a benign thumbs-up emoji appeared seconds later.

Étienne typed again. Are we still on for tomorrow?

It's why I messaged you. Most of the fittings are done.

Already?

Yep. And guess who's missing?

In my defense, I was out of town.

You have all the excuses. Meet me at one o'clock tomorrow at the address on the spreadsheet. I'll get Papi fitted, too.

I'll be there.

On time?

Étienne chuckled. That was more like the Rafi he expected. Yes. On time.

Good.

Étienne, who had been falling over with exhaustion, was now wide-awake. He'd see Rafi in less than twenty-four hours. As he paid the driver and tumbled out of the taxicab, he paused to consider this new feeling. The man could hardly stand him. Had Étienne turned into a person who was instantly attracted to people who weren't attracted to him?

No, that had never been his way. He thrived as much on being wanted as on wanting.

Étienne dragged his carry-on up the three flights of stairs to his apartment. But his mind was not with his luggage, nor had he spared the usual poisonous thoughts to the ancient elevator mocking him from the ground floor, challenging him to board again. He barely recalled putting the key in the lock and opening the door to his immaculate flat, which no one except his housekeeper had visited in the last two weeks.

All he could think about was the way Rafi had

looked at him in the elevator, all sweetness and compassion. Or the way he must have looked when he called him *brave*. Or the way it felt to have his mouth against his, to catch his breath as he breathed, to recall the taste of him as if their lips were still fused together.

Étienne scrubbed at his face. This wouldn't do. Rafi had made abundantly clear what the boundaries were and he would not be the one to overstep them again. But it was pleasant to imagine another reality where those boundaries did not exist, and Étienne could be free to express his desire exactly as he wanted to.

Chapter Eleven

Rafi

"I like it." Rafi observed his father as he turned on the platform that elevated him so the tailor, Mr. Sandovar, could adjust his tuxedo. Papi wore a replica of the one Rafi had sent to Étienne. "Watch out, lady-killer," he teased.

Papi laughed, the shaking causing Mr. Sandovar to pause in his work. After apologizing, Papi said, "We'll be here all day if you keep that up, Rafi."

"If you could lift your arms, please." The older gentleman pulled a pin from a cushion attached like a porcupine-shaped clock to his wrist. Papi did as he was asked, holding his arms out like a helicopter propeller. "Only a few more adjustments."

Papi gave Rafi a wink, to which Rafi smiled before glancing at his phone again.

"Don't worry." Papi lowered his arms at the tailor's quiet prompting. "He'll be here soon."

"He's late," Rafi complained, staring as the digital number changed, adding another minute to the time. Rafi had a terminal allergy to tardiness. "We had to take the train and we still managed to get here on time. What's his excuse?"

"Traffic? An emergency? *¿Que importa?* Even if he had arrived on time, he would have had to wait anyway."

"That's not the point," Rafi growled. "If you can't even count on someone to show up on time, then what can you count on them for?" He hated to have his time wasted and given the way their first encounter had gone, Étienne knew that. Rafi went out of his way to be as reliable as possible and did not understand why Étienne couldn't make the same effort.

"*Mijo*, don't be so dogmatic. Life doesn't run on a school-bell schedule. If you put your standards so high in the sky, no one will be able to reach them."

Rafi pulled a face when the shop door opened. Étienne sauntered in as if he was walking across a red carpet unfurled only for him.

"You look sharp, Enrique," Étienne said before turning his gaze on Rafi. His coat billowed open as he slid it off to hang it on the rack, revealing snug, black slacks, belt and shoes shined to a high polish and an impeccable blue-and-gray turtleneck that clung to the musculature of his chest. A platinum watch glinted from his wrist, contrasting perfectly with the overall dark hue of his outfit. Rafi had a baffling urge to reach out and touch the material of the sweater, which looked like crushed velvet smoothed over a swell of hard muscle. The thrumming of Rafi's heartbeat pulsed under his skin, a vibration he couldn't contain. He glanced down at his phone to keep from staring at Étienne.

"Like I was saying, you're late," Rafi retorted.

"Where I come from, I'm still on time." Rafi looked up to catch Étienne scanning him from top to bottom. He licked his lips, and the air around Rafi thinned to nothing. "Are you going to sentence me to detention?"

"Sentence you to… Wh-what are you saying?" Rafi stammered.

Étienne's eyes twinkled wickedly, which had a disastrous effect on Rafi's already stampeding heart rate. "Is that not what teachers do to children who are naughty? Send them to the headmaster's office to be lectured? Keep them after school to copy out their multiplication tables one hundred times?"

"Not in this century."

Étienne's laugh prickled across Rafi's already too-sensitive skin, the effect of the smooth, masculine timbre exasperating him.

"You wouldn't make it ten minutes in my classroom," Rafi practically growled.

An eyebrow shot up like a gauntlet being cast. "I was always the teacher's favorite. At least, for those who had the good humor to appreciate me."

"Guess I wouldn't be one of them."

"Guess not."

The clearing of Papi's throat interrupted Rafi's ready retort. "I'm done. Mr. Sandovar is ready for you."

Étienne walked away without a backward glance, leaving Rafi choking with annoyance. He wanted to argue with him, snap in half this thing that kept Étienne fixed in his thoughts and left Rafi in a perpetual state of heightened awareness. His mood must have been written across his face because upon Papi's return from the changing room, he studied Rafi for a long moment before speaking.

"¿Que te pasa, mijo?"

"Nothing."

"Doesn't look like nothing. Looks like a lot of something to me."

Rafi took a deep breath, shoving the phone he was worrying in his pocket. There were so many things he could say to his father, but none that he was ready to give voice to, even to himself. He went with the easiest, pettiest complaint, the one that exposed him the least.

"I don't like people disrespecting my time, that's all."

"Hmm," Papi responded. "Okay."

Rafi almost bit out a snide remark at his father, something he never did, when Étienne stepped out of the changing room and onto the low dais at the tailor's suggestion.

Rafi didn't remember his approach, but one moment, he was at his father's side, and the next, he was standing in front of the dais, staring up at Étienne. No one had the right to look as good as Étienne on an average day, much less in that tuxedo. Rafi needed to figure out a strategy to combat this fact, instead of getting flustered each time Étienne showed up.

"You like?" Étienne asked, his lips twitching with a barely suppressed grin.

"No. I mean, yes." Rafi wiped his mouth with the back of his hand, half expecting to come away wet with drool.

"Val did a good job choosing this style," Papi said as the tailor pulled the cummerbund snug around Étienne's trim waist. "Looks good on you."

Rafi's throat refused to allow speech to pass. He stood agog, like a block of granite, his eyes following the lines of Étienne's tuxedo as Étienne discussed its fit with the tailor. A fold of his cummerbund bunched and, as the tailor worked on the jacket, Rafi stepped forward in that same automated way and began to straighten it. It wasn't until Étienne's hand descended on his and went very still that Rafi became aware of their respective positions—Étienne like some modern iteration of a Greek god freed from marble, Rafi a diminutive Pygmalion at his feet, adjusting him as if Étienne were his statue, and his body was his to touch.

"What are you doing?" Étienne's voice was barely above an exhalation.

Rafi snapped his hand back. "It was wrinkled. I didn't want it to ruin the fit."

Étienne's eyes smoldered as they had that night,

burning with the knowledge of a secret only they shared. "Thank you."

The same look had ensnared Rafi and drawn him into a catastrophic decision that ended with their lips pressed together, giving way to the hot pleasure of each other's mouths with the anticipation that what could come after that kiss would be annihilating, an abandon Rafi knew he'd never return from.

If Rafi didn't control himself, he would step onto the dais and wreck them both just to get a taste of Étienne's mouth again, exposing his desire to everyone in the shop. It rattled at his insides like a bird trying to escape a cage.

"No problem." Rafi stepped away, turning abruptly on his heel and pacing to the end of the store on the pretense of looking at outfits that hung on perfectly shaped mannequins, each boasting the precise ideal male figure that stood incarnated on the tailor's dais. Rafi buried his hands in his curls, desperate to catch his breath, to remind himself of all the reasons why the way he felt was a pathway to disaster. Étienne was chaos in the body of one person and could make him lose the careful control he'd cultivated all his life, the control that had insulated him from the terrible things he knew awaited him if he gave in. And Étienne was Philip's best friend—the same Philip who was marrying his sister. He should be off-limits on the strength of that alone, no matter what designs his sister had.

Rafi despised feeling this out of control. He'd

never seen one good thing come from surrender. He knew this fact only too well.

A hand on his shoulder pulled him from his self-absorption. He turned to find Papi studying him. "Étienne offered to give us a ride home."

"Papi…" Rafi's voice was edged with the beginnings of desperation. But he pulled his thoughts back into order. He wanted to turn down the offer, but Papi would be so much more comfortable in a car instead of being jostled by commuters the way he had been on the way there. It would also turn a half-hour trip into a drive of only ten minutes, depending on traffic. He could make this small sacrifice for his father. It wasn't Papi's fault he couldn't get a grip on himself.

He cursed not having a driver's license, which was silly because he was not interested in owning a car. Not in the city, where insurance would wreck his monthly budget and parking was an exercise in martyrdom. But if it would keep him from constantly ending up in Étienne's car, then maybe it was worth considering.

Fitting completed, the drive home was less fraught than the one they took the night of Val's engagement party, mostly because Papi finally took the hint and let Rafi sit in the back, allowing Rafi to melt into the background. Papi and Étienne carried on a robust conversation that began with tuxedos, and meandered through details of Étienne's family life Rafi didn't know, like him having a sister with two children, or his elderly parents who lived with her. His father looked awestruck by Étienne when he talked about who he'd photographed lately. Rafi ground his teeth until his jaw ached. *Et tu, Papi?*

Except the biggest traitor here was Rafi. He couldn't get the way Étienne looked in his tuxedo out of his mind. And that image led to the treacherous memory he was trying and failing spectacularly to forget, the hard line of Étienne's body as they danced, the musk of his exertion mingling with his cologne and the smell of fresh-off-the-rack clothes. His shallow breathing when his lips hovered over Rafi's, waiting for the permission Rafi would later yank away like the coward he was.

Because in all his evasions and rationalizations, he was terrified of this thing that crept in each time he was with Étienne. Rafi was burning, while Étienne, who was as cool as ice, couldn't be bothered with him except to fulfill this collaboration, to offer up this singular labor of love to two people who meant everything to them.

Rafi couldn't wait to get out of the car and change his clothes so he could shoot hoops with Dariel and his friends at the community center, including whichever neighborhood kid showed up. A couple of hours on the court would set his head straight, maybe help cure him of his fixation on all things Étienne Galois.

Étienne pulled up to a spot in front of Navarro's under the recently fixed streetlamp, which was off in the midafternoon sunshine—the infuriating thing had been flickering for half a decade at least—and was out of the car and at Papi's door before Rafi's feet touched the ground. When Étienne winked, the whoosh of Rafi's blood rushing through him spiked in his ears.

So damned petty.

"Gracias," Papi said.

"A la orden," Étienne answered in perfectly enunciated Spanish. Rafi repressed the urge to roll his eyes.

Rafi stepped aside to let his father get his footing on the curb. He made sure to keep his eyes away from Étienne's smug expression, focusing instead on getting the hell out of there.

"Are you in a hurry?" Étienne teased when Rafi tried to get away with a wave goodbye and a quick escape.

"I, ah, I have a basketball game this afternoon at the community center. My friends will be waiting and unlike other people, I don't like being late."

Étienne stared at him and Rafi could have sworn he saw a faint echo of that moment on the dais. "A formal match?" he asked finally.

"Pickup game for whoever shows up."

Papi was smiling all the while at Étienne as if he was his new best friend. "Next time, you should join them. They are always short a few players."

"Do you play?" Étienne asked Papi.

"Oh, no. But I like to watch. I have a good friend who lives near there."

Rafi narrowed his eyes at his father. His friend was probably none other than Ilaria Rossi. Of course. Rafi was the only one who couldn't figure out his romantic life.

"I happen to have a set of gym clothes in the trunk. Running shoes—probably not the best for basketball, but no matter." Étienne clicked the fob to open the trunk. "This will be perfect. I haven't moved in a few days and my body aches."

He had to be kidding.

Étienne was all systems go with Papi's suggestion. Dammit. Rafi's decompression point, the very thing he was looking forward to in the hopes of getting Étienne out of his mind, was predicated on him not being present. This was the very opposite of decompression.

"I'd hate to throw off your schedule." Rafi hoped Étienne might catch a clue. "We're never sure how many people will show up besides my group, and sometimes it's only the kids."

"Even better!" Étienne clapped his hands, a laugh lacing his every word. "I only need somewhere to change."

"Come inside," Papi said. "You can change in my place while I make coffee. I might even come with you."

Rafi's felt his lips disappear to nothing. He had never wanted to throttle his father more than at that moment.

"Great," Rafi muttered, reaching for his manners. Étienne in his neighborhood. Étienne on the court. Étienne covered in sweat. Étienne's bubble butt bouncing around the court.

Rafi's internal scream kept him company as he followed them inside.

Chapter Twelve

Étienne

The impulse to accept Enrique's invitation had come out of nowhere. A part of his brain warned him to stop, turn around and go home. But the other part couldn't resist poking at Rafi and making him squirm. Plus, it would have been impolite to reject the older man's obvious suggestion. That was not how Étienne was raised.

Étienne followed Enrique up the walk and inside the building to his flat, Rafi's eyes tracking them. Étienne gave him a wave, which Rafi haltingly returned.

Enrique unlocked the door of his apartment and gestured at Étienne to follow him. "Coffee? Or do you prefer tea?"

"I don't want to make Rafael late."

"He won't be late. I want something warm so you can share a cup with me. Or not, it's up to you."

Étienne relented. "Coffee, please."

Enrique nodded, clearly pleased. "My bedroom is at the end of the hall, bathroom inside. You can change there."

Étienne followed his directions. Opening the door, he found an immaculate space, decorated with old-fashioned, heavy wooden bedroom furniture. The four posts were thick and varnished to a shine, the mattress high, making the room feel stuffed. On the wall hung a picture of a woman who was pretty and round-faced like Nati, with hair a few shades darker but nowhere near as brown or curly as Rafi or Val—that had been their father's contribution. The end tables were covered with doilies, upon which rested elaborate, cast-iron lamps. A glass tray of cologne, combs and a metal cup half-filled with small change sat in the middle of a bureau. There wasn't a speck of dust anywhere, making Étienne afraid to breathe in the intimate space.

The bathroom was also carefully decorated as Étienne changed, he thought of his own apartment, and his sister's house, the way they all carried pieces of their homeland with them wherever they went. The knitted bomba dancer in a traditionally flared red dress hiding a roll of toilet paper under her skirt, the framed photograph of a coqui frog sitting on a dew-beaded banana leaf, the coordinated greens, reds and oranges that called to mind sunsets stream-

ing through the mountains and glittering light on
the beach. It took Étienne back to the beaches he'd
combed with his friends, sprinting across scalding
heat to reach the water. His heart ached for the Jacmel of his youth, the beautiful chaos of a town forever dappled in light and art, before that terrible
night had taken so much from them all. The night
that changed everything for him.

When he finished changing his clothes, he followed the aroma of brewed coffee to find Enrique
already sipping from his own tiny cup.

"How do you take it?" Enrique asked, pouring out
a stream of black liquid into a similar cup.

"Milk and sugar, please," Étienne answered, taking a seat at the small breakfast table.

Enrique placed the espresso cup on a tray together with sugar and cream pots and set it in front of
Étienne before taking a seat. He remembered Rafi's
reaction to the water and fruit, warmth flooding him
at the memory of their bickering, the odd satisfaction of it. He was also acutely aware that Rafi had
not come upstairs yet, and his absence prickled at
his awareness.

"Rafi should be up soon," Enrique said with uncanny prescience.

"Probably avoiding me," Étienne answered, un-
thinkingly.

Enrique laughed. "Don't mind him. He can be
abrupt, but he is a good boy." Enrique smiled, an
older, more informed version of his son's smile. "I
know why he stays here. He thinks if all my children

leave, I will be alone, and he doesn't want me to stay alone. He is more afraid for me than I am for myself."

"My parents live with my sister since my father's stroke. It has not been an easy recovery."

"Oh, yes. With two children, she must be busy all the time."

"It's nonstop."

"My parents lived with my sister until they both passed away. Mi Gabriela…" Enrique paused. "My late wife had a beautiful heart. She tried to persuade them to come live with us here in the US, but they did not want to leave the island."

Mi Gabriela. Étienne's heart gave a single, painful thud at the simple phrase that said so much. A woman nearly fifteen years gone, a woman he still considered his.

"So we sent money to help take care of them and went back when we could," Enrique continued before releasing a huff of air that sounded like a laugh, his fingertips drumming on the smooth wood of the table. "Listen to me, talking nonstop."

"I don't mind." Étienne's voice went husky with emotion. Rafi was the spitting image of his father and his mind had begun conflating his father with Rafi, opening a yearning in him to share something meaningful with this man. "I think I would enjoy hearing your stories."

"I have so many of them. That's what happens when you get old."

"You are not old," Étienne protested.

Enrique laughed and Étienne saw it. The glint of

his wedding band as he smoothed a hand over his chin. He had seen Rafi's expression when his father mentioned his friend and wondered if this friend wasn't of the romantic variety. Étienne hoped fervently it was. He understood why Rafi couldn't stray far from his father. Someone like him should not be alone.

"Papi?" Rafi's voice came through the door of the apartment.

"Aquí," he answered, guiding Rafi to the kitchen with his voice. *"Hize café,* if you like."

"Excellent brew." Étienne downed the last of his coffee.

Rafi stepped into the kitchen, a bubble jacket under his arm, beanie fixed on his head. He wore an unzipped gray hoodie, a thermal, long-sleeved sports shirt underneath, and a pair of black sweatpants with a designer insignia emblazoned on one leg. Taut bumps and valleys of muscle rippled beneath his workout shirt. Rafi's eyes flicked to Étienne's snug sweats, lingering on his thighs before flitting away, and Étienne secretly thanked his past self for always keeping a clean, fashionable set of workout clothes in his car.

"No, I'm good. Filled a few water bottles for us, too." Rafi pointed at the gym bag he carried. "Ready?"

Enrique hid a yawn behind a closed fist. "I think I'm going to stay home and take a nap. I opened the restaurant earlier than usual this morning." He stood, Étienne following suit.

"What about your friend?"

"My...yes. I forgot. She's at her sister's house this weekend. You boys have fun. Oh, and Rafi?"

"Yes, Papi," he asked, his voice squeaking.

"Why don't you two stop by Pepe's after the game?" He directed his explanation to Étienne, the mischief in his eyes bringing a smile to Étienne's lips. "Pepe's family is from Cuba, but they are descended from Chinese immigrants to the island. The food is a fusion of both and it's excellent."

"You want spring rolls, don't you?" Rafi asked, shaking his head at him.

"Four, if you don't mind. And *arroz frito.* Bring—"

"Extra soy sauce. Yeah, I got it." Rafi gave his father a kiss on the cheek. "You think you're slick."

"I am, *mijo.*" He clapped Rafi's shoulder. Étienne offered his hand to Enrique, but he gently pressed it away.

"Strangers say goodbye like that. But we aren't strangers." He pulled him in to leave an air-kiss on the cheek. "I heard the duck is good, but it's not good for my cholesterol."

"Neither are the spring rolls but that's not stopping you, is it?" Rafi complained.

"I will try it on your recommendation," Étienne said to Enrique.

"Good. Now go. I want to take a nap."

Rafi observed his father with a barely repressed smile before he led Étienne out of the apartment. Étienne pointed to his car, but Rafi shook his head. "The weather is decent. If it's okay, I'd like to walk."

"Your leg?"

Rafi glanced down at his knee. "Much better."

Étienne buttoned his coat, which was far too formal for his outfit but did a good job of protecting him from the bracing weather. He glanced at Rafi out of the corner of his eye, the smile hinted at in his father's apartment not entirely gone. "Your father seems like a kind man."

"Papi?" Rafi nodded. "The best, but I'm biased, you know?" He hesitated before adding, "I think he likes you."

Étienne wanted to say something flippant, like of course, everyone likes him. But he didn't want flippancy between them. He longed for something more authentic. "He has the wisdom of someone who has been through a lot, yes?"

"Yes. His family had large land holdings in Puerto Rico before they lost everything. He went from being a spoiled rich kid to working the fields, then leaving home to start all over again in the US." Rafi glanced at him, before turning to look forward. "It was polite of you to accept his invitation."

"It was more than manners," Étienne said quietly. "I like him, too."

"I can see that." Rafi furrowed his brow, as if he'd been handed an equation he couldn't easily solve. He opened his mouth, seemed to think better of it, closed it, then spoke again. "I've been playing with this group since I was in high school. We trash talk each other a lot. And the teenagers are even worse, but they don't mean anything by it. They get carried away with the game."

"I was a teenager not too long ago."

"Nah, you're ancient."

"I most certainly am not," Étienne exclaimed, prepared to launch into a diatribe against the cultural assumption that anyone over thirty was somehow diminished by age, but a glance at Rafi's twitching lips brought him up short. "You're teasing me."

"Serves you right for coming late to today's fitting."

"Are you still bothered by that?"

"No," Rafi answered and Étienne sensed the honesty behind his answer. "Well, initially, I was. But that was only because it reminded me of an old assumption I'd made about you."

Étienne's eyes grew wide. "Which assumption was that?"

"That you don't care. I can confidently say that's not true."

Rafi frowned, a crease appearing between his eyebrows that Étienne would thumb away, if he could. "My dad is a good judge of character," he said, more to himself than to Étienne. Rafi speaking to him in this way was a 180-degree turn-around from his earlier dismissal and it left Étienne disoriented.

They arrived at the community center. Étienne had hardly been mindful of the walk and would be hard-pressed to find his way back to Rafi's building without the help of his GPS.

"Is this where you play?"

Rafi's attention snapped into focus. "Yeah. It's

the old community center. Been here since as long as I can remember."

Étienne studied the worn exterior of the two-story building before them. The polished windows covered the entire first floor, interspersed with graffiti on the brick between the windows, while the second floor was dotted with cubicle windows. Adjacent to the building was a basketball court with a group of boys already shooting hoops, sending a basketball into a weather-worn net. Posters hung, some intact, some in shreds, along a chain-link fence, blocking bits of the moving action like a filtered pattern of sunlight.

Étienne pulled out his phone and took several photos from different angles, carefully adjusting the filter and lighting before taking more. Rafi watched him with rapt curiosity. When Étienne had taken a dozen, he pulled up the photo gallery and showed Rafi. Rafi scrolled, nodding as he studied each photograph in detail. "I've been playing here since I was a kid, but your pictures make it look—" Rafi waved his hand until he found the words "—unconventionally beautiful."

The unexpected affirmation swelled through Étienne. He had an idea and paced around a confused Rafi until the lighting was just right. He raised the phone. "May I?"

Rafi blinked several times. "My clothes don't even match."

Étienne shifted from behind his phone. "Your clothes hardly matter. Relax and I'll take the pictures." He gave small indications about when to smile, where to look, what to shift. It was the part of the game Étienne loved the most—trying to catch that one true thing about a subject. He found it when the light fell on Rafi so perfectly, he looked other-worldly. Étienne made sure to snap as many photos as he could until the moment was gone.

"Here." Étienne showed him the photo gallery. "I like the last ones."

Rafi studied each one. "It doesn't look like me. The way you caught the light…" Rafi looked at him with something like awe. "You did that with only a phone camera?"

"It's a very good phone camera." Étienne smiled, almost as proud as when he'd been nominated for the International Photography Awards. "But it would have been better with my professional camera."

"I hate myself in photos," Rafi confessed, a blush that wasn't caused by the brisk weather prettying his skin, and Étienne gave in to the impulse, photo-graphing that, too.

"Why'd you do that?" Rafi said.

"You have the potential to be a mesmerizing sub-ject."

Rafi dipped his head and Étienne was charmed by the gesture. "Is this why you do it? Take things that aren't perfect and make them look good?"

Étienne gave a snort. "No. I do it because it's the only way to stop time."

Rafi hand shook as he handed Étienne his phone. "That's too deep for me. Let's go lose a basketball game."

"Speak for yourself!" Étienne retorted. "I never set out to lose. I'm terrible at it."

They went inside to check in with the attendant at the front desk before crossing out to the courts.

"Rafi!" came shouts as several young men became aware of his arrival. Étienne remembered a few from Val's engagement party—the married couple, Dariel and Noah, one of Rosario's cousins, Caio. Simon, the baker, and Javier, their brother, were already in action, passing the ball back and forth. Étienne felt the familiar excitement of meeting new people creep in. But this also felt important, like something he wanted to get right. For so many reasons that also included maintaining positive relationships for Val and Philip's sake, he wanted them to like him. He consciously turned on the charm and prepared to meet this group of people Rafi seemed to care for so much.

Chapter Thirteen

Rafi

"This is Étienne. You guys remember him from the engagement party?"

"Yeah, Philip's best man." Dariel asked Étienne, "You play?"

"It's been a while, but yes," Étienne answered.

Rafi pretended to ignore the way Caio was checking Étienne out, not even trying to be chill. The sweats that hung off Étienne's hips and accentuated the swell of his butt made him look model-fine. This should have been a nonissue for Rafi. He had lots of good-looking friends, but he wasn't thinking about any of them nonstop. Plus he'd spent every minute of his existence lately telling himself how *not* into Étienne he was. It was only a matter of time before someone flexed and went for him. The man was gorgeous, had a great personality, knew how to respect the older generation, was a good friend to Philip, had Rafi's family eating out of his hand and...

What was his point?

Rafi snatched the ball out of Javier's hand and raced off, dribbling around players, not liking the turn his mind had taken. He needed to keep his head in the game and ignore anything that did not directly pertain to kicking ass on this court, especially with his leg not being one-hundred-percent. He was one of the shortest guys out here, but he was the fastest. He couldn't have thoughts of Étienne messing up his game.

"You can be on my team." Caio waved Étienne over to his side of the court.

Rafi resisted rolling his eyes, then sent the ball to Javier. They quickly decided on teams—Javier and Rafi together with Dariel and one of the kids from the neighborhood, while Simon, Noah, Caio and Étienne made up the other squad.

"You ready?" Rafi paused to ask Étienne. Before he could say another word, the ball was gone and in Étienne's hands, the *clop-clop-clop* against concrete reverberating through the shuffle of basketball shoes as he dribbled past him.

"Too slow, *viejo*," Étienne snarked at Rafi as he made a two-point jump shot.

"Hey!" But why was Rafi surprised? Étienne was good at everything. Cursing, Rafi went after him, fouling him when he slammed up against Étienne's unbelievable rock-hard body. Rafi backed away, the echo of Étienne's chest still imprinted against his own. Étienne took the free throw and missed, Caio catching the ball as it fell away from the basket and made an airball from the other side of the court.

"You thought, big guy!" Rafi recovered the ball on the drop and bypassed Dariel, who was guarded by Noah from behind, and passed it to Javier for a point. Dariel stood with his hands in the air, face aghast.

"I was right here!" he shouted.

"So was your man." Rafi pointed at Noah, who was strutting as if he was somebody.

"On the court, there is no loyalty," Étienne said. They circled each other, neither able to break away. Breathing hard, their bodies were glazed in sweat, and maybe, Rafi wasn't trying hard enough to get away from him.

And on and on they played, words flying faster than the basketball. Rafi was sure they'd play better if everybody shut the hell up, but the ribbing was too much a part of their routine. Étienne had slid right in, a little too good at all of it—the playing and the burns. Except when he directed them at Rafi, they didn't sound like smack talk at all. They sounded like little promises suffused with layers of meaning. Even with Caio trying to get into Étienne's space, or watching him appreciatively when they stopped for water breaks.

But that wasn't Rafi's concern. Didn't even notice all the times Caio stopped to check Étienne out. Or the way Étienne preened at the attention. Damned man was an inveterate flirt, and it grated on Rafi's nerves.

Rafi sighed, strolling over to where Caio and Étienne were still talking. Rafi considered inviting Caio to Pepe's, but put the idea on ice. Caio could do his own damn work.

Rafi placed a hand on Étienne's shoulder and, holy hell, it was like touching a live wire. "Hey, we have an errand to run, remember?" He let his hand fall before it became too comfortably perched on Étienne.

"Oh, right." He turned back to Caio. "Nice meeting you."

"Same. Best-man planning, right?" Caio asked.

"You know it." Rafi waved to his friends, leading Étienne out of the community center. He handed Étienne his coat before zipping himself in. His leg twinged, but nothing that hampered his movement. The evening was brisk and while the sun had been sweet, that brief, warm reprieve could do nothing against the snap of evening cold.

"Nice group," Étienne said as they headed back in the direction of Navarro's, with a quick detour two streets before to Hanua Cubana, or Pepe's, as Papi referred to it.

"Some were nicer than the others," Rafi complained, feeling like he'd swallowed battery acid. Caio was his friend and, he guessed, so was Étienne. Those two flirting with each other shouldn't have felt so annoying.

"You mean Caio? He was friendly. But you would know better than me, since he is your friend."

Rafi shrugged. "You'll have to talk to him to find out."

Étienne's silence was heavy and thoughtful. Rafi hadn't lied. It was Étienne's business who he hooked up with. They'd shared a moment, but the moment was long gone.

"If it's all the same to you, maybe I will call him."

"I have his number if you want it." Rafi took out his phone to search for the contact, but Étienne stopped him.

"Don't trouble yourself. He gave it to me already."

Rafi nearly dropped his phone. "He did?" he asked, raising his hands as if in surrender. "Guess you don't need me playing matchmaker."

Rafi turned, trying for a saunter, a black energy exploding from an angry place that gnawed at him. Étienne's hand wrapped around his arm, tugging him back. Rafi turned and glared at him, ready to say something cutting.

"I'm not calling him yet." Rafi stopped. Étienne had said *yet* but not *never* and Rafi's stomach twisted in response. "Does it not matter if I do?"

"No," Rafi answered, his voice straining for a normal tone. "It doesn't."

Étienne studied him and Rafi saw what he saw—a somewhat sweaty guy in a bubble jacket and work-out clothes, trying to stare him down in the middle of the sidewalk, probably doing a terrible job of intimidating anyone. "Are we going to pretend this does not exist?"

Rafi's face went numb. "What do you mean, *this*?"

"I meant precisely what I said." Étienne's hand on his elbow was like a slow-burning pulse. Étienne was so close, he could smell his sweat and expensive cologne, and Rafi, for no good reason, wondered what his skin would taste like.

No, not again. He couldn't lose control. He knew better.

"It's not…there is no *this*."

Étienne shook his head, the heat of his breath purring across his skin. Rafi turned his face up like a moth seeking light, ready to batter itself against the heat until it caught fire and turned to ash. "It's okay to not want it. But it's not okay to deny what is there."

Rafi wanted to say please, to beg him to…what? Let him go? Pull him in? Make him remember? Make him forget?

"I can't…think when you're this close," Rafi said between gritted teeth, the truth breaking out of him.

Étienne stared at him, dazed. Thankfully, the universe took pity on them both and Rafi's phone rang.

Rafi pulled away, fishing the phone out of his pocket. Val's name flashed across the screen.

"I have to take this." He set off in the direction of the restaurant as he answered, but she barely let him get a greeting in edgewise.

"I missed an appointment with the caterers, and I've seen so many venues, I can't tell them apart anymore." She took a deep breath as if confessing to a crime. "I might be in over my head."

Rafi didn't want to tell Val that he'd told her so. Val was one of those people who had to hit her head against a wall to accept it was solid. "I'll help you find somebody."

"I've wasted so much time already."

"Only a few weeks." Rafi hated when Val got upset, even if she was responsible for her own predicament. His automatic instinct to problem-solve kicked in. "We can make up the time somehow. First priority is to find a wedding planner ASAP." Rafi had a hand in his curls, tugging hard as he thought about where to start.

"If I may…" Étienne's voice came from beside Rafi. He held his hand out, his expression smug and a bit too self-satisfied for Rafi's taste.

Rafi gave a slight shake of his head, not understanding. Étienne raised an eyebrow. "Trust me."

"Val, hold on." Rafi handed Étienne the phone.

"Thank you." Then, "Val! How are you? Yes, I heard… I know, it's challenging…of course…"

Rafi listened to Étienne's side of the conversation, imagining Val's rapid-fire responses until he handed the phone back to Rafi, who looked at him in askance before speaking into the phone.

"Well?"

"Étienne recommended a wedding planner. He saved my life."

"I heard that." Rafi glanced at Étienne, who had walked a few feet away to talk on his phone.

"It's not a done deal until he speaks to her, but…" Val laughed softly. "I feel a million times better. Thank him, please. Papi said you were having dinner at Pepe's. Treat him. I'll pay you back."

"As if I'd take money from you."

"But—"

"Don't worry. I was planning on treating him anyway."

She dropped her voice. "Étienne's great. I hope you see that."

Rafi glanced over at Étienne, who had ended his own phone call and was waiting patiently for him. "He's not too bad. But don't tell him. He has an ego as big as an Airbus."

"Stop it," she laughed. "And thank you. Both of you."

"It's what family does, right? Have each other's backs?"

"Étienne is practically family, too."

"So everyone keeps telling me. You guys are obvious as hell."

Val squealed, actually *squealed. "Te quiero mucho."*

"I love you, too."

Rafi ended the call and turned to find Étienne firing off a text. When he looked up, he gave a thumbs-up, which coincided with a message from Val in the same instant.

His friend agreed to meet with me!

Rafi sent her a series of fireworks emojis before lifting his eyes to Étienne. Étienne had already composed himself, but the dark intensity that had blown all of Rafi's thoughts from his mind had not disappeared entirely from his expression, especially when he made no effort to hide the way he raked his eyes up and down Rafi's body before holding his gaze.

"Thanks. If you hadn't done something, she would have kept spiraling."

"I told you I would do anything to make their wedding a success."

Rafi looked away, the earlier moment lingering on him like knots that refused to loosen. He had to bring this back around, play it cool until they reached status quo again. "Come on. My turn to treat." When Étienne tried to protest, Rafi put his hand up. "It's the least I can do after…all that."

"It's my job as best man."

"Half your job. I'm technically the other half of this operation."

"We're a team, now?" Étienne's surprise was genuine.

The awkwardness was getting to Rafi. He wanted a reset, wanted the night to go the way it was supposed to, not weighed down with impossibilities. "Yeah. Come on. We're both hungry."

Étienne sniffed himself. "I am not suitable for public consumption."

"Trust me, Pepe's seen worse. The food is amazing, but the ambience isn't exactly going to win him a Michelin star."

Étienne chuckled at this and Rafi breathed again, the mood of earlier dissipating. "I will order this duck your father recommended. I have a feeling he will want one of us to report back on it."

Dinner went by quickly, without any near misses for repressed libidos. Turned out playing basketball, solving wedding snafus by phone and resisting the temptation to climb your sister's best man like a giant oak was enough to induce a massive appetite in anyone.

The glazed red Formica table was soon littered with empty plates, half-filled glasses of lemon water, discarded straw wrappers and crumpled wax bags that once held metal cutlery. The soy-sauce bottle sat at Étienne's elbow the whole meal—Papi wasn't the only one who liked his food a little on the salty side.

Rafi set his plate aside, using a napkin to wipe the corners of his mouth and his fingertips of the remnants of his *arroz frito* and Chinese-Cuban five-spice roasted pork.

Étienne toyed with his still-wrapped fortune cookie, his plate long since polished. "Your father was right about the duck. Excellent choice."

"You keep saying that." Étienne worrying the cookie had him curious. "Give me one. Let's see what our future holds."

Étienne tossed him a small bag before tearing open his, his strong fingers proceeding to demolish the cookie onto a napkin, sliding the paper out amidst a shower of crumbs. Étienne cleared his throat. "'Seize the moments but make them last.' Well, that's a lot of generic nothing."

Rafi tapped his thin thoughtfully. "I don't know. Sounds like they read you."

"How?" Étienne crossed his arms in quiet challenge.

"It's like you have this carpe-diem thing going on." Rafi leaned forward. "You went through something traumatic in your life, and it taught you that you need to seize the day. Grab the moment because life is too short to waste any of it. But in doing that, you forget to slow down long enough to enjoy those moments. So in the end, your joy is fleeting, not the kind that lasts."

Étienne studied him with a serious expression that made Rafi fear he might have offended him. But without warning, his face split into a grin. "Nice try, *sòsye*. Let's see what yours says."

"I don't know what you called me, but I'm right."

"What's your word? *Brujo?*"

"Yeah, that's it. I'm a seer." Rafi carefully opened his bag, the vanilla aroma curling sweetly out of the package. He slid his paper out, making sure not to break the delicate cookie.

"You're going to eat it, man, not put it on your mantel," Étienne said.

"Patience, my friend, you will learn." Rafi ignored the way Étienne rolled his eyes. He read the paper. "'Fear and desire—two sides of the same coin.'" He glanced at Étienne, whose own attention was fixed on him. Rafi dropped his eyes to the slip again. "I want my money back. Mine isn't as cool as yours."

"The cookies are free." Étienne rested an elbow on the table, leaning on his hand, watching Rafi. "I am inclined to think yours is quite accurate."

"I'm not afraid of anything."

Étienne shrugged, his face holding an expression that warned Rafi he was in for a teasing. "Want my thoughts?"

"No. But that won't stop you, will it?"

"No, since you did not spare me yours." It was Rafi's turn to roll his eyes as Étienne spoke. "I think you are afraid of many things. Nothing physical—you would slay those if they appear."

"Like a superhero, right? Let me guess—Spider-Man?"

"Perfect choice," Étienne laughed. Rafi knew it was because of his build, the way people always told him he looked younger than his actual age. "No, you are afraid if you let things fall out of order, you won't get them back under control again. And this, more than anything else, would be catastrophic for you." Étienne straightened, unable to keep from letting his hands speak for him. "That's why you line everything up, put things in their proper place. Otherwise, if things come apart, it might mean the end of the world as we know it. Extinction-level event. The destruction of human civilization…"

"Yeah, okay, I got the idea." Rafi shook his head, trying to hide how uncomfortable he was with Étienne's observation. "I don't know what to say."

"You could agree that I am right."

Rafi shrugged. "If I did, there wouldn't be any room left for you, me and your ego at this table."

Étienne's lips twitched before he burst out into a full belly laugh that drew the attention of the handful of customers in the restaurant. It was infectious and soon Rafi was following suit, laughing at this absurd human being who made him feel things he didn't want to feel, and want things he absolutely shouldn't want.

Étienne took a sip of his water, then said, "I think that's the first time I've made you laugh."

"That's weird, because sometimes you're actually funny."

"I know!" Étienne practically boomed. "You are a tough audience." His laughter dried up and he continued in a more serious note. "You should laugh more often."

Tension prickled through Rafi, rolling through his chest, his belly and his groin in equal measure. He slid out of the booth. "Papi's spring rolls should be ready. I'm going to pay so we can get out of here."

Étienne gathered his things as Rafi put space between them, letting the routine of paying for food give him the moment he needed to get himself right again. There had been too much truth in Étienne's observations. Rafi had abandoned all the rules he'd erected to keep Étienne from affecting him, and now he had to build them back up, brick by brick. He'd need time to do that, and it couldn't happen with Étienne around.

It was after nine o'clock when they finally made it back to Rafi's building. It felt both late and early, and Rafi struggled with the simple fact that he didn't want any of this to end.

Étienne hooked his gym back more tightly over his shoulder. "Thank you for dinner. I'm going directly home. Don't want to risk anyone else sniffing me."

"You don't smell bad."

Étienne gazed at him but said nothing.

Rafi offered him his hand. "Thanks again for helping Val out."

Étienne gently pushed his hand aside and stepped close enough that Rafi could see the individual hairs of his short beard. "Strangers say goodbye like that. But we aren't strangers, are we?"

Étienne lowered his cheek to Rafi's, slow enough that a rejection of any kind would have been possible. But Rafi let his eyes close and held still as Étienne left a kiss low on Rafi's cheek, above his jawline. He could have pulled away, *should* have pulled away, but held still as the kiss sank beneath his skin, nestling there, turning the world into pure sensation. Lights flickered behind Rafi's eyelids, while the pulse of his heavy heartbeat radiated through him. Everything ached and he couldn't ignore the dull throb that told him he was growing hard. God, Rafi wanted Étienne, the realization plowing through him so forcefully, he could taste it.

Étienne pulled back with the same agonizing slowness, pausing over Rafi, watching and waiting as Rafi's eyes slowly opened. Everything inside him screamed at him to stop because only danger lay on the other side of giving in to Étienne. Yet they were so close, he had only to lift his lips to meet the way they had once before.

But Rafi folded his desire deep within and held fast against Étienne, against himself, his insides twisting with competing impulses. Perhaps Étienne noticed his struggle because he pulled back, the moment draining away, leaving only another bright memory of longing behind.

Étienne's face shed the intensity of their near kiss to let a smile, however tremulous, shine through. "I'm in town for a longer than usual. Best to book the bachelor-party venue while I'm here."

Rafi was aware of how fragile, how out of control, his feelings were. He needed to go home before he did something he would regret. "We'll talk soon."

Étienne hesitated before getting into his car. Rafi listened to the engine purr to life and pull out, a last wave before he clutched his things and escaped down into the apartment, slamming the door shut behind him, as if he could outrun his feelings. As if he could bar them from following him inside and wreaking havoc on him.

Chapter Fourteen

Étienne

Étienne took extra care while trimming his beard after a sleepless night. The day he'd spent with Rafi ran on loop in his head and kept him from finding much-needed rest. Étienne had been too close to kissing that gremlin and needed to stop setting himself up to be constantly rebuffed by Rafi and accept that nothing was going to happen between them.

There was also Philip. He was like a brother to Étienne, and Val was coming to mean the same to him. This thing with Rafi was too close to risk those relationships. It was bad enough his parents did not accept his choices; he could not risk the rejection of his friends, too.

He looked at the contact on his phone. Caio was a

good-looking man who had shown an uncomplicated interest in Étienne. He did not possess Rafi's penchant for overthinking, and he would not upset the connections Étienne so cherished. Étienne gripped his phone, his thumb hovering over the buttons, poised to strike.

He shoved the phone in his pocket instead. It never turned out well, going out with one person to get over another. Feelings didn't work that way.

He thought of his recent exes, the beautiful, ambitious Malena, or gentle, kind-hearted Jean, partners he should have felt more for, but could not. People who, in theory, Étienne should have fallen in love with.

Instead, he was agonizing over a man he should not feel anything for, a person for which anything more than friendship had the potential to strain important connections. A person who would not follow through on their indisputable connection, and refused to even acknowledge it.

He pushed Rafi roughly out of his mind, determined not to waste any more time on him. He was due at his family's house for dinner, which he attended as often as his schedule allowed. His mother had tasked him with buying a few things at Nanette's Grocery, which he now juggled in a paper bag.

Étienne knocked on the door of his sister's apartment, adjusting his plain black sweater—not one of his bespoke creations made for his long body and wide shoulders. He'd once worn a striped baby blue and navy-colored dress shirt crafted from a bolt of batik he'd bought from a wonderful artisan during a photoshoot in Jakarta. It had barely survived the meal, falling victim to his niece's and nephew's grease-covered fingers. At five and seven years old, they were endowed with the supernatural ability to target and smear only the finest of his clothing. He had learned his lesson.

Deidre answered the door, a little girl in pink tights and an oversize green sweater appearing from behind her legs.

"Tonton!" Jonielle squealed.

"My little Jo-Jo. Look what I have for you." Étienne pulled out a LEGO pirate ship. "You see, when you build it, the plank will extend and inside—"

"Gra-a-a-a-an-n!" Jonielle erupted, taking the box, and racing inside to show her grandmother. Deidre tried to stop her but Jonielle whipped past her mother and tore around the corner, her shouts trailing behind her like streamers of pure joy. Another, smaller child appeared, face eager and expectant, replacing Jo-Jo at his mother's side.

"Jacques." Étienne smiled, kneeling to look him in the eye. "Did you think I would forget you?"

He shook his head, stifling a giggle behind chubby fists so that only his enormous, brown eyes were visible.

Étienne took out a LEGO Duplo set, this time of an excavator, more appropriate for his younger age. "Now, am I allowed to come inside?"

Jacques nodded quickly before dragging his haul in the direction his sister had gone.

Deidre took the paper bag from Étienne's arms, stepping aside to let him in.

"Their father and I don't exist. They prefer their grandparents to everyone else in the world." She spoke in Creole, which, together with the smell of his mother's cooking and the sound of Jonielle's gleeful voice, wrapped him in the cozy comforts he associated with his family. It was not the home they'd grown up in, the one that haunted his dreams and insinuated itself into his unguarded moments. That home was gone, a memory to be cherished or avoided, when necessary. But this building was also his home because it was where his heart now lived. Where his sister cared for their parents and nurtured a family of her own.

"I would prefer the company of my *granmè* and *granpè*, too, if they spoiled me as much as they spoil Jo-Jo and Jacq."

Deidre stepped forward to give him a kiss on the cheek before leading him toward the kitchen. "You bring them a toy each time you visit! You are as bad as they are."

"Uncle privileges," Étienne retorted.

He followed his sister to the kitchen, where his parents were engaged in one of their usual playful bickering while Jo-Jo and Jacq tore through the packaging of their toys. Deidre shuffled them into the living room.

"Ah, but who taught you how to cook?" Papa said from his seat at the kitchen table, where he was peeling a pile of vegetables.

"Don't start that," Manman retorted. His parents had always cooked together since as long as he could remember, and the competition to outdo the other was just as old. "Your *poul nan sos* will never live up to mine."

He pointed at his wife with the potato peeler. "I see I will have to teach you another lesson, eh, woman?"

"Papa, I would not provoke her if I were you," Étienne interjected, giving his father a pat, followed by a kiss on his head. Papa was as tall as Étienne, but the stroke of several months ago had impacted his mobility, requiring that he use a cane to walk. In a house with two rambunctious children, he had to be extra vigilant. His mother, who was independent and still drove, got him to all his biweekly physical-therapy appointments in addition to his other medical visits as his condition continued to improve. Étienne offered material support, but Deidre put in the time and energy each day to make sure their parents were thriving.

Étienne turned to where his mother stood before the hot stove, stirring the spicy rice that would accompany the chicken.

"Manman, here are the things you asked for."

Manman's cheeks were flushed with the heat of the stove, but she was still immaculately made up, hair coiled and styled, delicate gold jewelry like glitter on her dark skin. She pulled him down and left a kiss on his cheek.

"Perfect. I am precise with my ingredients."

Papa scoffed at her words. "Doesn't help."

"Scoundrel," she hissed, snapping him with the corner of the dish towel. Étienne had gotten that easy laughter from her, while his father's competitive nature had descended on both his children. "I ran out of epis." She nodded to a medley of garlic, celery, peppers, onions and herbs partially chopped on a cutting board. "Your sister was helping me, but she has to chase those ruffians down." She said this with none of the irritation one would expect from having children screaming underfoot. "When you put the groceries away, would you finish blending it?"

"Of course," Étienne said, moving around the kitchen to put away the things his mother had requested before washing his hands and dicing the vegetables on the cutting board. It was equivalent to *sofrito*, the thought inviting Rafi to his mind and he wondered if, among the many tasks Rafi had been taught to do in his family's restaurant, this had been one of them. The idea of cooking with him, wearing silly aprons and preparing a meal together, seized him with the force of a premonition, and instead of chasing the fantasy away, he indulged it. What harm could a simple fantasy do?

Deidre's voice tore through his thoughts. "You cannot be in here while the adults are cooking, Jo-jo," Deidre scolded behind a scampering Jonielle, who was clutching a figurine in her hand to show her *granpé*.

Deidre's husband, Paul, followed with Jacques under his arm. "Étienne!"

"Paul!" Étienne tried to give him a proper greeting, but the child he carried was a squealing, writhing mass of movement.

"I'm going to get them dressed and take them to the park. They need to burn energy outside the house," Paul said. "Sorry to come and go like this."

Étienne waved him off. "We'll talk later."

Paul carted them off while Deidre caught her breath.

"It's nonstop," Deidre huffed, pulling her braids into a loose ponytail. "Sometimes I think of hot gluing them both to the wall to keep them from charging into something. Not as glamorous as your life."

"It's work, like any other," he said, and felt the mood in the kitchen instantly change.

"It does seem like fun, for now," Manman said.

Anxiety over the same, tedious conversation rise in Étienne. "Just because I like what I do does not make it any less exhausting."

"Is it stable?" Papa interjected. "I used to love to paint but I studied to be an engineer because I knew I would always find work."

"I have been employed with the same magazine for years, and my private commissions are more than I can handle. I am well-compensated, as you know. I never skimp on anything you need."

"We know," Manman said soothingly. "We worry about you, that's all."

Étienne sighed. "I cannot spend my life defending my career choice. I'm not going to become an engineer at my age. Why must we always have this conversation?"

Deidre patted her father's shoulder, forestalling

his retort. "I think it's exciting to have a world-famous photographer in the family. We can't all be business analysts and engineers, yes?"

"Thank you," Étienne said. Maybe, with repetition, this line of conversation would eventually die out, though he was not optimistic, even with his sister's support.

Étienne's phone vibrated in his pocket. He pulled it out and glanced down at it, his heart skipping a little when he saw Rafi's name flash across the screen.

"I must take this." He switched into English and excused himself to go into the hallway before answering.

"Hello…" Rafi's voice was tinged in uncertainty, or maybe that was Étienne, projecting his own state.

"Rafi. How are you?"

"It's only been a few days so not much has changed."

"Better that things are the same and not worse."

Rafi cleared his throat. "Since you're home for a while, maybe we could start planning the bachelor party before you leave again."

Étienne was still reeling from the unexpected call. "That sounds good."

A pause, then he asked, "Are you free today?"

Disappointment at having to turn Rafi down washed through him. "I'm having dinner with my parents. What about this week?"

Étienne heard tapping in the background and realized Rafi was probably using an e-planner. "I'm not free again until Saturday."

"Then Saturday it is. Come around six. I'll be sure to pick up the griot so you can finally try it."

"You're as bad as Val. All she thinks about is food." The small laugh that came across the phone pulled an answering one from Étienne.

"Food is life. I take it seriously."

"No wonder you two get along."

"You don't seem to be under duress when you eat."

"Who doesn't like a good meal?" Rafi huffed. "But you guys take it to the next level."

"Would you prefer a hot dog from the corner cart?"

"Hell, no. I'm good."

There was a pause, in which there didn't seem to be more to say, and yet Étienne was hesitant to let him go. He should—he'd already gone far enough with Rafi, crossed too many boundaries, except he couldn't stop wanting to cross more, cross them all, and it made him feel foolish.

"I'll see you soon."

"Yes," Étienne said. "And do try to be on time. We know you have a problem with punctuality."

"Keep telling yourself that."

Rafi went silent and Étienne sensed the undercurrent connecting this moment to that other one they were both trying so hard to ignore. Étienne thought he should offer Rafi an out, say goodbye but…he didn't. He was having a beast of a time letting him go, even if a shared silence was all he was offering.

Oh, Bondwye, he wasn't supposed to feel this way.

"I should go," Rafi said finally.

"Good night, Rafael." After signing off, he leaned his shoulder against the wall, replaying the conversation in his mind, reveling in the delight that Rafi had called him, that they would be meeting soon, much sooner than he had dared to hope. A hand on his shoulder yanked him back from his thoughts, making him jump.

"Who was that?" Manman asked.

"Woman, are you trying to kill me?" He rubbed the shock from his chest.

The melody of her laughter washed over him. "No one is trying to kill you, silly boy. But that did not sound like work."

"As it happens, I was speaking to Val's brother. Rafael."

Manman's eyes blazed with curiosity and the wheels of her brain visibly turned. Étienne was in trouble. "Philip's fiancée's brother?"

Étienne had to be careful. His mother had the uncanny ability to sniff out secrets, wherever they hid. "He is helping me with my best-man duties. Philip thought it was a good idea, given my schedule."

"Philip!" She clapped her hands. "He was here for a visit last week." She leaned in and whispered, "You are liking this Rafael boy, yes?"

"He is hardly a boy. And how did you go from an innocent phone call about wedding planning to me liking him?" Étienne asked, dabbing at his forehead with the napkin he always kept in his pocket.

"I know my son," she said, her grin full of self-satisfaction.

"For your information, we are just friends."

She raised an eyebrow and Étienne felt the cross-hairs lock on him. "Do all your friends make you sweat?"

"Manman!"

Manman tilted her head coyly. "Ah, well, you can never have too many friends. What does he do?"

Étienne closed his eyes, feeling the familiar pressure build in his head. "He teaches high-school math."

"A professor! I like that."

"No, Manman, not…he's a teacher. At the high school."

"Does not matter. Is he a nice gay boy like you?"

Étienne said in his most patient voice possible, "I'm bisexual. But, yes, he is a nice gay boy. Gay man," he corrected quickly.

She petted Étienne, smoothing her hand over his shoulder and back the way she used to when he was young. "I get confused sometimes with all these labels when they are all describing the same thing."

"What is that?"

His mother smiled at him. "The different ways people love each other, yes?"

It was impossible to be annoyed with her.

"I remember Malena. Such a lovely woman but you were not taken by her. I knew it would not last."

"You never said anything."

"It's not a mother's job to live her children's lives.

These are things you must understand for yourself." Manman crossed her arms, watching Étienne. "And Rafael? What is he like?"

"Difficult," he responded before he could stop himself.

"Like you?"

"I am not difficult. I am the easiest person to get along with."

"Yeah, okay," his sister's voice came from the kitchen.

Étienne started. "Is there no concept of privacy in this house?"

"You have been living in the US too long," his father chimed in.

His mother suppressed a laugh behind a balled fist as they returned to the kitchen, where Deidre was enjoying a coffee with her father, a reprieve from her tiny demons. "So is he handsome?" Deidre asked.

"Unbelievable," Étienne muttered to himself before answering. "Passingly so."

"More than passingly so, if I remember correctly," Manman chimed in.

"Show me a picture," Deidre pressed. "Come on, Camera Boy, you must have one."

Étienne growled but pulled out his phone to appease her, angling it when he found the ones he took of Rafi outside of the community center. "Happy?"

He cringed as his mother and his sister oohed and aahed over Rafi's photograph. "He looks like a professor!" his mother exclaimed.

"A professor?" His father leaned in, all aglow with interest.

"A math professor," his mother said, elbowing her husband in the side as if Rafi were a lottery ticket they'd all won.

"No, not…" Étienne began as they talked rapidly among themselves, dissecting everything they could about a man they barely knew from a photograph of him wearing workout clothes. "Oh, forget it."

"Invite him over," his mother said.

"How can you like him if you met him only once?" Étienne asked in exasperation.

"He has kind, intelligent eyes." She pointed at her own, as if Étienne couldn't imagine what she was talking about.

"We are Just. Friends," Étienne said, enunciating clearly, hoping they would get the hint. "You are the one who said not to fish too close to home!"

"And since when have you ever followed your mother's advice? You like him, I can see it. Bring him home," Manman said with finality. "I have always enjoyed meeting your friends."

Étienne sighed. Why did he think he had any autonomy as an adult? "As soon as it's convenient. We are busy with Val's wedding."

"That's my boy. Now help me set the table so the food will be ready when the little ones come back. They are looking forward to watching a movie with their *tonton*."

Étienne had promised them they could watch a film of their choice after dinner, in the hopes of giving his sister and her husband a break before Étienne returned to his place. His mind would not be on the film, but on Rafi. Étienne had always introduced his friends to his family. How many times had Philip come with him, to the extent he visited them on his own, as if Philip had extended his circle of family to include them, as well? His parents saw Étienne's friendships as a sign he was thriving, confirmation that their decision to leave the island for the good of their children had been a sound one.

Except that, despite every wise instinct and sage admonishment against getting involved with Rafi, he was coming to mean more to Étienne than a friend, and he would not be able to hide that from the incisive gaze of a family who knew him all too well. His heart would be exposed in all its forbidden desires, and if he wasn't careful, they would come to light.

Chapter Fifteen

Rafi

Rafi arrived at Étienne's apartment as arranged, offering in hand, examining it for any signs transport might have damaged it. At least it hadn't fallen victim to gravity as he once had.

He pressed the buzzer, awaiting the sound of the lock unlatching. After more than a minute, when the sound didn't come, he tried again. And again. Rafi stared at the offending bell as if glaring at it might intimidate it into letting him in.

Rafi had confirmed their appointment the night before. So why wasn't Étienne here?

He pressed the button one more time for good measure, but the results were the same. Rafi took a seat on the steps, setting his cheesecake carefully next to him, and pulled his phone out. He typed out a simple I'm here, then shoved his phone in his pocket and stared moodily at the traffic. He tried to keep what his father said in mind, that not everything runs on a bell schedule, but the irritation wouldn't die away. He had been so excited, more than a session of party planning could justify. Obviously, that excitement was one-sided.

He exhaled. The afternoon sun was melting into evening. He shivered at the chill seeping in from the concrete step he sat on and the frigid air nipping at his ears. He glanced over at the cheesecake. At least it would keep.

"I'm here." Étienne's voice came from the sidewalk. His smile was bright and his steps chipper, which, despite Rafi's irritation, quelled his mood somewhat.

Rafi raised an eyebrow as he straightened, taking the pie in hand. Étienne held two plastic bags filled with takeout containers. "The restaurant was running behind on their orders."

"Hmm," Rafi said, stepping aside to let Étienne pass.

"I can feel you judging me, Mr. Punctuality."

Rafi's scowl softened. "Only a little."

Étienne's laugh pulled Rafi forward. He was having a hard time holding on to his annoyance. Rafi held the door for him, bags rustling as they cleared the threshold and made their way upstairs.

"My friend Nicola has a small restaurant around

the corner with her wife. They make the best Haitian food. A little like your Hanua restaurant."

"Mom-and-pop places are the best," Rafi said.

"Or mom-and-mom in this case. Here we are." Étienne let him inside. A dizzying haze of heat and tempting aromas enveloped him—the subtle heft of men's cologne, the spices wafting from Étienne's bags and the crisp aroma of soap and shampoo, like someone had recently showered.

They removed their outerwear and Rafi had to put a hand against the wall to steady himself. Unlike his usual impeccable outfits, Étienne was wearing a simple, V-necked blue sweater and gray sweatpants. He slipped his bright, white-socked feet into a pair of leather house slippers, the kind Rafi's grandfather might've used and should've been dowdy, but on Étienne, managed to be vintage and elegant.

And glasses. Étienne pulled out a pair of thick, black-framed reading glasses that he perched primly at the end of his nose.

Étienne caught him staring and gave him one of his wicked grins. "Do the glasses surprise you?"

Rafi swallowed hard. No one had a right to look that good in casual clothes. "The glasses…yeah."

"I'm farsighted and I want to admire what you gave me." Étienne's smile split his face in half, and he reached for Rafi's cheesecake.

"I made it last night."

Étienne raised an eyebrow and plucked up the edge of the box, inhaling before beaming brightly, and it made Rafi's stomach go all fluttery. "You re-membered. It will go perfectly with our meal."

"You promised griot." Rafi busied himself with arranging his own things on the peg at the entryway.

"And I always keep my promises. Guest slippers on the shelf. My mother always said, to avoid catching a cold, you should keep your feet warm."

Rafi removed his shoes, then slid his feet into the set of Burberry-patterned slippers lined with fleece he'd worn the first time he visited. "My parents were more like 'take your shoes off, you have no idea what you're bringing in from the street.' They didn't care if your feet were cold. The just didn't want us dragging dog poop from outside."

Étienne snorted as he carried everything to the kitchen. Rafi had been too distracted by pain and annoyance the first time he'd been in Étienne's apartment to admire it properly. He took care to examine the stunning photographs in frames of various sizes arranged on the walls. Interspersed on shelves lining the walls were curios such as carved gourds, bits of bas-reliefs and paintings in multiple styles. The decor was a visual tour de force, so bright and overwhelming, it was easy to mistake the arrangement as haphazard. Upon closer examination, Rafi perceived the intention—primary colors punctuated by patterns that picked up those same shades and passed them about the room. Controlled chaos and harnessed joy, much like the man who lived in it. A man who didn't hide from life's messes but embraced

them with both hands and used them to fuel his inexhaustible energy.

Rafi could be so blind sometimes.

He followed the sounds of cutlery and glasses
clinking together. Used Styrofoam containers were
scattered around the narrow countertop. Étienne
seemed to take up all the remaining space. Aside
from the mess, the kitchen looked like it could've
been taken from any in a Caribbean home, with
splatters of orange and yellow against bright, white
walls. Overflowing potted vines crawled over the
large window, framing the fire escape and a cloud-
blotted sky beyond.

"Can I help you with something?" Rafi asked.

Étienne glanced behind him, his framed eyes rak-
ing over Rafi in a quick assessment that was probably meant to be subtle, but made Rafi feel like warm
water was cascading over his skin. Étienne's eyes
snapped up to his before he handed him a bowl holding utensils, glasses, napkins and a tablecloth. "How
are you at setting a table?"

"I was practically born inside of a restaurant."
Rafi balanced everything with the ease of long prac-
tice. "I got this."

Rafi made his way to a dining-room table that
sat four and deftly set everything up. On a whim, he
picked up two candelabra, each sculpted with three
images of the same woman—one veiled, one unabashedly sensuous, one in the shape of a mermaid.
Gorgeously wrought, they shared the same flaring
hips and slim waist. Rafi set them down carefully, as

if he could injure them by rough handling. Étienne brought out the hot dishes, dumping cloth trivets unceremoniously onto the table.

"Sorry," Étienne muttered as he set down a bowl of the hot griot, and a mix of black rice and beans that looked like *arroz congri,* but which Rafi recognized as *djondjon* rice. Étienne returned to the kitchen and brought a plate of *tostones* and a baked dish that Rafi didn't immediately recognize.

"Is that baked mac 'n' cheese?"

"*Makarowni au gratin.* My mother made it. I am a dismal chef, I'm afraid." Étienne tucked his glasses away, which Rafi mourned, and pulled out a chair for Rafi before taking his own. He visibly started at the candelabra in the center of the table. "Did you place them there?"

Rafi shrugged, flushing as if caught in the act of doing something forbidden. "It's such a nice dinner, I thought…"

Étienne got up and went to rummage in the drawer of a nearby credenza. He returned with two candles and a silver candle lighter. He placed them in the holders and lit them.

"You are right. A dinner such as this one deserves something beautiful."

The now-darkened sky opened and rain clattered against the window, rendering the candles resplendent against the night. Rafi was back on the veranda of Aguardiente during that summer, with lanterns and fairy lights punctuating the evening. The air lulled by music and the rushing river, and Rafi, heedless of everything except Étienne beside him.

Étienne's voice pulled Rafi away from that dangerous memory into a more dangerous present. "Eat. There is nothing worse than cold food."

Rafi smiled, thinking of something similar his mother always said to get the family to the dinner table. Étienne caught Rafi's smile and returned it with an unabashed sweetness that left Rafi aching. Rafi focused on the food instead.

"This looks so good." Rafi inhaled, the braised, citrusy aroma, vinegar and spices tugging at his appetite.

"Nicola wishes you bon appétit."

"Thank her for me." Rafi took a bite of pork, rethinking his irritation at coming out here, injuring his knee and enduring the unsettling headiness that was Étienne Galois. "I can taste the sour orange and parsley. Is that garlic?"

"Yes, but not so much that it overwhelms the flavor of the meat. You have a good palate."

"I picked up a few things while helping Val in the kitchen," Rafi added. He savored the familiar tastes of his family's kitchen recombined in a way that made the flavors fresh and delicious. When he tasted the alternate crispy and smooth texture of the au gratin, Rafi closed his eyes in appreciation. "Tell your mother I had nothing but good things to say about the au gratin. It's perfect. Everything is perfect."

Étienne smiled as if the accomplishment was his own and Rafi recognized the pride-by-proxy a person could have when others recognized the good things that could come from your people. Silence, easy and companionable, descended as they ate. When they were done, Rafi brought up his ideas for the bachelor party.

"A barhop weekend?" Étienne asked.

"Only the one night, but we'd start with the groomsmen checking in and having cocktails at the hotel before herding everyone to dinner. I have a list of restaurants and bars I sorted by type and reviews that we could visit. The weather is usually mild by then. Do you think Philip would like that?"

Étienne scrubbed at his short beard. "I believe he would."

"There's even a *Star Wars*-themed bar in the area. Did you know he and Val went to a convention and cosplayed as Jedi?"

Étienne's laugher washed over Rafi in luxurious waves. "Val indulges Philip in everything."

"I think it's a mutual indulgence, to be honest."

Étienne grew thoughtful. "An indoor pool? Or spa?"

"A hotel with an indoor pool where we can have brunch and watch a match the next day before sending everyone home. *¡Perfecto!*" Rafi grinned as he tapped notes into his phone.

Étienne leaned on his hand, watching him. "You missed your calling as a party planner."

Rafi set his phone next to his plate. "The pool was your idea."

"If you arrange the itinerary and reserve dinner,

I will book the hotel and plan the cocktail party and brunch. Fair split?"

Rafi nodded. "I'll add it to our—"

"Spreadsheet. Yes. It has proven helpful. Words I never thought I would speak aloud." Étienne stood to collect the dishes and Rafi followed behind him into the kitchen.

He was assaulted all at once—Étienne's towering nearness, his fresh smell of cleanliness, the lingering spices of dinner. Rafi had an unexpected urge to bury his nose in Étienne's back and inhale deeply. Lost in a minifantasy of smell and heat, he stepped too close to Étienne, who turned at the same moment, nearly knocking a plate from his hands.

"Caramba!" Rafi exclaimed as Étienne barely rescued the plate from crashing to the tiled floor. He freed Rafi's hands of the second plate and set them both on the counter so there was nothing between them but mere inches of electrified air.

"I'm sorry." Rafi was painfully aware of the heaviness of his body, tension pulsing through him.

"They're only plates," Étienne whispered.

Every sound he made, every exhalation, fell on Rafi like lashes of heat, scalding him.

"I…" Rafi had something flippant on the tip of his tongue, but Étienne's thumb came to rest between his eyebrows and smoothed the space there.

"You are always thinking, thinking, thinking." Étienne's voice was hypnotic. "Never a step taken without calculating the consequences."

Rafi shook his head. "That's not true."

"Isn't it?" Étienne traced a thumb over his eyebrow, hitching on his cheekbone before sliding down his face. Rafi needed to cut this off and step away. It was still early enough to return home on his own steam now that they'd made some decisions about the bachelor party. Except Rafi hadn't come to settle their endless plans, all of which could have been resolved with a video chat or email, without requiring him to come all the way out to Étienne's apartment. Rafi had known all this and come anyway because he'd wanted to see Étienne, wanted to hear his voice, and feel his laugh prickle over him in person.

Étienne's thumb was on Rafi's jaw, his large hand cupping his chin, light enough that Rafi could pull away if that's what he wanted.

Étienne lifted Rafi's face up. "Tell me one time you did something without thinking about it first."

Rafi's breath came out, ragged and broken and barely enough to sustain him. "You know."

Étienne gave Rafi's chin a slight squeeze. "I want to hear you say it. I want to know that I did not dream it."

Something deep in Rafi sundered, splitting in half those flimsy threads of self-control and duty and fear that he'd believed could hold him together, keep him intact and away from this aching want.

"Say it," Étienne insisted, his fingers firm, but still gentle.

"When—when we kissed."

Étienne nodded. "We kissed and then, you started thinking again and you ran away."

Rafi wanted to say it wasn't so much the thinking but the terror that all he wanted would tear him apart, make him lose his precious control, inviting catastrophe into his life.

Instead, he said, "I know I was a coward. I thought…" He hadn't thought anything. He'd feared an unpredictable outcome, unable to trust what would come after because he was tired of being wrong, and paying for it. *Fear and desire—two sides of the same coin.*

Étienne nodded, as if satisfied. "And if I kiss you now, will you run away again?"

Rafi struggled with a response that sprang from a deep well of self-protection, a place so exposed and fragile, even the thought of touching it made him want to collapse into himself. But he pushed through it. "No."

Étienne's eyes darkened, swallowing the electric lights of the kitchen, the soft flicker from the candelabra, until he was the only point of brightness in Rafi's vision. And Rafi closed his eyes to it, focusing on the flood of Étienne's breath over his skin, the soft lips that grew more determined as they pressed against his.

A small, needy sound escaped Rafi's lips, and in that opening, Étienne swept in, his tongue a swirl of teasing heat. Some last fortification within Rafi struggled to stay upright. He slid his arm around Étienne's neck, dragging him in, and he returned Étienne's invasion with something fierce and desperate of his own. Because he had never been afraid of Étienne, but of himself, of what he might become if he gave himself up to this.

Étienne pulled Rafi against him, deepening the kiss, and Rafi pressed him back against the counter in answer, hips slotted on hips. Étienne's gasp of surprised left Rafi feverish. He shivered when his own hard erection pressed against Étienne's and some last barrier gave way. He swirled his hips, forcing another gasp from Étienne's lips.

"You are a revelation," Étienne said, wonder and surprise lacing each word. Étienne slid his hands down Rafi's sides until they landed on the swell of his ass, palming the curves he found before hiking Rafi up against his own body.

Rafi broke away first, breathless and bruised and aching to have Étienne beneath him, spread out like his own personal feast. He fixed Étienne in his firm gaze. "This is a terrible idea."

"It is."

"As long as we both agree." He balled the front of Étienne's sweater and pulled him in for a bruising kiss. His restraint, the constant denial of what he wanted, had turned into a hunger to possess Étienne in the most incontrovertible way. Rafi scrabbled at the hem of Étienne's sweater, sneaking beneath to splay his fingers and drag them across his hot skin. He thought of all the ways he could have Étienne and nearly froze with the competing possibilities of taking him all at once, or lingering over him in slow, methodical consumption.

"Come." Étienne half spoke, half hummed the

word against his lips. He led him out of the kitchen, pausing only to pinch the flames of the candle between his forefingers and thumb. Rafi captured those fingers, kissing away the sting of heat, the smoky flavor of a spent wick, watched Étienne's eyes grow heavily lidded, heard the hiss of air that sounded like his name tumbling from his lips.

Chapter Sixteen

Étienne

Rafi's soothing kisses on his fingertips turned to sucking while Étienne looked on in awe. Rafi in the grip of arousal was like nothing he had experienced. And Étienne had a fair bit of experience. With Rafi, he had imagined a fraught, almost virginal surrender, clawing through gnarls of denial and overthinking. Not this bold, eager sensualist who couldn't stop touching and tasting him, who commanded each step and propelled them toward Étienne's bedroom. Their progress was painstakingly slow as Rafi paused to leave a line of kisses up the sensitive side of Étienne's neck, tumble against the wall to grind their hips together and scrape his nails along Étienne's skin. Étienne hiked Rafi up, forcing his legs around his hips, and with fused lips, carried him the remaining steps through the threshold of his bedroom until they tumbled gracelessly onto the bed.

An *oof* from the impact and a short burst of shared laughter disappeared under the serious business of kissing. Accustomed to Rafi's sharp barbs and quick retorts, this version of him, eager and unfolding beneath Étienne's weight, disoriented and focused him at once.

Rafi broke away, turning his face to catch his breath before slipping his hands beneath Étienne's sweater, up his ribs, to thumb his nipples. "So what are you into?"

The words took several seconds to process before Étienne could formulate an answer. "You. I'm into you."

Rafi gave him one of those smiles Étienne always craved from him—unabashedly happy with a side of lasciviousness. A twist and a slide and soon Rafi was hovering over him, thighs on either side of his, the panels of his open shirt swaying, framing their bodies.

Rafi dipped his head to kiss Étienne again before he tugged at his sweater, getting it up and over him, then paused to run his hands over Étienne's chest. He yanked off his shirt the rest of way, the fabric billowing as it floated to the floor. "Don't move."

Étienne liked this take-charge spirit and threw his hands up in surrender. "I am at your mercy."

Rafi's breath visibly stuttered at his words. Eyes dark and skin flushed, he applied his hands, then his mouth, to discovering the secrets and valleys of Étienne's body. Rafi worked methodically over him, thumbing the hard, oversensitive nipples until Étienne moaned with the burn of it. Rafi's tongue chased the path of his fingers as he found the swirling calyx of Étienne's belly button, and kissed the quivering cuts of Étienne's abdomen, the tops of his thighs that appeared when Rafi rolled his sweatpants and boxers down and off.

Then Rafi stopped, flicked his eyes up to Étienne's and waited.

Étienne hiked himself up onto his elbows, curled his fingers behind Rafi's neck and pulled him in for a kiss that felt like the consummation they were building toward, a wordless encouragement to continue, before he released Rafi.

"You like this. Taking control," Étienne said.

A moment of tension flickered through the taut lines of Rafi's body. "It's not about control."

"Isn't it?"

Rafi fingers dug hard into Étienne's thigh and Étienne liked the way Rafi used his body to anchor himself. "Would it be a problem if it was?"

"For now, no." Étienne buried his fingers in Rafi's hair, running them over his scalp until one thumb rested on Rafi's lips. Rafi's eyes fluttered closed and he took his thumb in his mouth, suckling it. Étienne's words came in a whisper harsh with desire. "As long as you are willing to surrender, as well."

Rafi took this in and nodded solemnly before returning to his travels, sliding and kissing until he was between Étienne's legs. Étienne watched Rafi drop kisses on his thighs, his knees, ankles and toes, avoiding the place where Étienne so desperately wanted him.

"Where are you going?" Étienne gritted his teeth as Rafi, nose and lips burrowed in the join of his thigh, pulled back without touching Étienne's erection, which arrowed hard and aching over his belly.

"You in a hurry?" Rafi retorted, holding Étienne's eyes before taking him in hand, sliding his hot palm over him. Étienne's breath evaporated at the long-awaited sensation, but his eyes flew open when Rafi's mouth followed and all his protests about control and surrender drowned in a barrage of sensations concentrated on the slide of Rafi's tongue.

"Bondye mwen," he muttered when Rafi licked his way up the thick vein. Étienne balled the bedsheets as Rafi applied himself to the task of driving Étienne cross-eyed with pleasure. When, with a perfect slide, Rafi engulfed him and swallowed him down, Étienne lunged his hips in desperation to make the sensation last.

But this was Rafi, between his thighs, mouth so quick with rejection now full of Étienne and the thought pushed him over the edge. His orgasm broke out of him, and it was all he could do to not keen his release into the air.

Eyes glittering with victory, Rafi kissed his way up Étienne's body. He was still wearing his jeans, the top buttons loosened from Étienne's incomplete efforts to get them off, and a moment of intense vulnerability overwhelmed Étienne—naked and spent beneath a partly dressed Rafi. As if reading his mind, Rafi pulled back, quickly undoing his remaining clothes. Still groggy from his release, Étienne was not too far spent to admire Rafi's body, tight and lean with muscle, slim waist and strong legs.

He pushed the sluggish remnants of exhaustion from his body and reached for Rafi, crushing his lips in a kiss, pulling that same delicious, needy sound from him.

"Come here," Étienne said, flipping Rafi onto his back, capturing and pinning Rafi's hands above his head. Rafi's eyes darkened as tension pulled his body taut again.

"Cherie," he pleaded between open-mouthed kisses along Rafi's neck. "Let me pleasure you."

"It's hard for me to…let go," Rafi stammered, his breath ribboning out of him in shallow gasps.

Étienne released his hold on his hands, dragging his nose down his chest until he brushed his hard nipple, covering it with his lips and licking it to uncompromising hardness before lifting his head again. "Stop thinking."

"I…"

"Stop."

Rafi scraped his nails along Étienne's short beard. "Make me."

Étienne's rumble of laughter reverberated where their skin touched. He nipped at Rafi's tight belly before covering Rafi's body with his own.

Chapter Seventeen

Rafi

Étienne's words, rough and sexual, pulled Rafi out of his head. He wanted this so much, he was choking with the desire for it. He wanted to give pleasure, wasn't entirely prepared to lie back and receive it. He wanted to be the driver, control the scenario, control *himself*. Surrender was something that often eluded him. He could still taste Étienne, the salty flavor of his submission, and envied the ease with which Étienne gave himself up to it.

Étienne's hands slid over him and Rafi ached to get closer, until Étienne's large hand wrapped around his hardness and stroked, slow and sure. Étienne bit into his shoulder, holding them both in place. Rafi used to know words, used to know how to say things like "please" and "don't stop," but the circuitry that made such things possible had fused in his brain, and what fell from his mouth were garbled moans and grunts that might have been anything but conveyed only one solitary desire—*don't let me go.*

And Étienne didn't. He stroked and kissed and fondled him. Crushed Rafi's body with his weight until they were slick with sweat, and after a long interval of sliding against each other, Étienne buried his head in Rafi's neck, humming with mounting satisfaction. Words had deserted Rafi, but Étienne was overflowing with them.

"I didn't know it would be like this with you," he said, the words raw and jagged. "When I first saw you, I knew it would be good but not like this…" Étienne pressed a kiss to Rafi's neck, sliding a hand over his belly, fingers sending currents of fire as they explored and prepared Rafi, dizzying him with their rhythm.

It was everything Rafi resisted and everything he wanted. The struggle to hold back was old and tired, and *yes* fell out of his mouth, over and over. Étienne dragged him to the edge of the bed, making his nest between Rafi's thighs, stretched wide around those enormous shoulders. Legs pressed against his chest, Étienne flicked his tongue over every aching inch of him and further.

"Yes," Rafi repeated, as if it was the only word he knew. He held himself still, stifling his natural resistance. Étienne lifted his head to look at him.

"Are you okay?"

Rafi nodded. "Please," he choked out. "Don't stop."

It felt as inevitable as breathing—featherlike lips and tongue as hot as fire. A pause to search for the clear bottle of lubricant Étienne poured over his fingers. Rafi made no pretense of participating in his unraveling. Étienne had relieved him of the ability to do anything more than hold on as the storm threatened to wash him away. He was in an unfamiliar place—asked to do nothing more than to *be* and discovering that it was one of the most difficult thing he'd ever attempted.

Étienne's mouth engulfed him, a hand stroking, a slow finger easing into his heat, curled in a delicate but determined caress in search of that spot that would undo him. Rafi couldn't control the pooling heat that was causing him to clench at the edge. He was helpless before it and ordered his convoluted, overheated mind to shut up and just feel it.

The final caress of a second finger sent his release careening through his body, the spasms so strong, they were almost painful. Étienne swallowed it all until nothing remained but Rafi's cries.

Rafi wanted to linger like this, sprawled under Étienne, inhaling the scent of them, but Étienne was already in action, smoothing a towel from who knows where over him, cleaning him carefully. It was a sweet, tender gesture that moved Rafi and, unraveled as he was, overwhelmed him. He bit back the threat of tears, still in enough possession of his impulses to not surrender to raw emotion, but awash in more feeling than his body knew how to contain.

Rafi registered Étienne's arms, strong and steady, pulling him against his chest, a chuckle against the back of his neck, probably of smug satisfaction because Étienne would always be Étienne, whispering sweet nothings in Creole as he accompanied him into an irresistible sleep.

The smell of coffee slowly brought Rafi awake. He stretched, relishing the sweet aches and sore muscles that came with a long night of good sex. Awareness snapped into place like a picture suddenly gaining focus and Rafi's body betrayed a multitude of reactions—hard and ready, but also hesitant and shy. The memory of how they'd spent the night before, of how bold Rafi had been in giving himself to this growing need between them, chased away the last dregs of sleep. He reached over in search of Étienne and found…

Nothing.

Rafi shot up, uncovering the pillow with the faint indentation of Étienne's head still pressed into it, and roughed up the blankets as if Étienne might've gotten lost in the folds of the duvet. In the past, he'd woken to find his partners gone before morning and he'd always hated how empty it made him feel. As if he'd done something to chase them off.

Rationality asserted itself. He was in Étienne's apartment, not his own. Therefore, the likelihood that Étienne might slip out and disappear, leaving Rafi alone in his house, made no sense.

And then there was coffee. Divine, aromatic coffee that curled around him. For there to be coffee, there had to be someone around to make it.

After throwing on his T-shirt and boxers and tending to his needs, Rafi followed the smell and was assaulted with the memory of being carried through this same corridor. He shook it off before he became uncontrollably turned on again, and found Étienne, coffee cup in hand, resting his forearm on the jamb of the windowsill, the guava cheesecake open on the table next to him. He had on his sweatpants and socks—his only concession to the cold—and every fiber in Rafi's body shifted at the sight of so much Étienne on display. He looked hand-sculpted, someone a Renaissance artist might replicate in marble.

Étienne turned at his approach. Upon seeing Rafi, decidedly less like David and more like a rusty cherub spouting water, he gave him an enormous smile that made linear thinking an impossibility. Rafi tried to relax, returning his smile with a shyness that immobilized him.

"I have been waiting for you."

Étienne pulled him into a hug, the heat of which spread through him slow and thick. A glance out the window revealed what Étienne had been staring at—a park in the middle of a traffic circle, leafless trees ravaged by the cold, a small fountain that had been shut off. The reminder of winter sent an involuntary shiver through Rafi. He hadn't felt cold— not last night, lost in Étienne, not this morning as he made his way across Étienne's apartment to find himself enveloped in his strong arms.

"Do you know what I miss most about my island?" Étienne asked when he pulled back.

Rafi shook his head, dazed by the newness of being with Étienne in this way. Intimate, without any barriers. Without protections. "No."

Étienne smiled, kissed his forehead and pointed outside. "The mornings. We always woke to the smell of coffee grown in the mountains and bought fresh from the market." He handed Rafi his cup, which he took, savoring the strong flavor swirled with milky sweetness. "I've never smelled anything like it here in the US."

"Maybe what you're remembering isn't the coffee but the smell of home," Rafi said, observing the glittering frost that blanketed everything beyond their window.

"You're right." Étienne pointed at the coffee. "Is this okay? The coffee?"

"Everything's perfect."

Étienne grinned before pouring more coffee from the carafe. Rafi sliced the cheesecake, placing wedges on the plates he found there, then handed one to Étienne in exchange for the hot brew. "There was always my grandmother's fresh bread waiting for us every day when she was still alive." Étienne continued his recounting, pausing to take a bite of cheesecake. "This is delicious."

"When I made it, I didn't intend it as a breakfast food."

Étienne leaned in, giving him a coffee-and-cheesecake-flavored kiss. "This is a special occasion." Étienne winked, taking another bite.

Rafi took a long draught of the coffee to cover his stupid smile of pleasure.

He handed it back to Étienne. "Mami had toast with a boiled egg sprinkled with cumin powder waiting when we woke up. She made coffee, but not for us."

"Why?"

"She believed if we drank coffee when we were young, we would stop growing." Rafi swept a hand over himself. "I did what she said, but it didn't help."

Étienne let out a laugh that shook his entire frame, bringing out a smile of Rafi's own.

"You are big where it counts," Étienne said when the laughter had dwindled away.

Rafi flushed with embarrassment…and a primitive sort of pride. "I, uh…"

Étienne's eyebrows flew up. "No, I mean, of course. Proper proportions and all."

"I got it." Rafi enjoyed Étienne's discomfort. The moment surged through him, the ease of being with Étienne, how very little everything else mattered but this.

"I meant that you are big where it matters. Your heart…" He placed a large hand over the left side of Rafi's body, where his heart had picked up its pace in reaction to his touch. "You are a good brother, a kind son, a loyal friend." The hand resting over Rafi's heart slid with lazy familiarity over his shoulder and up his neck. Strong fingers twined through Rafi's hair. "And a generous, giving lover."

Étienne used his thumb to angle Rafi's head up, smiling as his lips descended. A sound only Étienne could pull from him escaped the kiss, sharp as ice and needy as hunger. Étienne tasted like coffee and the frosty morning that was slowly brightening into a frigid day. He kissed Rafi the way he did everything else—deeply, savoring each lick and bite. Rafi took it all in—the rough sensuality of his short beard, the fade that tempted him to haul his fingers up through curls that scraped against the pads of his thumbs. And Étienne's body, all exposed lines and hard edges, against which Rafi was held, iron wrapped in velvet. Étienne rocked against him, the insistence of his erection an echo of the hunger of the night before.

Rafi pulled away, gripping Étienne's shoulder, breathless and bursting with want. "Étienne… Maybe I should…"

"Stay." He pulled Rafi flush against him. "We have a bachelor party to plan."

"We did plan…a little."

Étienne moved a curl that had tumbled over Rafi's forehead. "Not every detail."

Rafi took a step back, unease flickering through him. The strangeness of this moment assaulted him at once—Étienne's apartment, the newness of having spent the night with him, the complete upheaval of all his certainties. The terror that he might have made yet another bad decision, with disastrous consequences. This instinct to escape and center himself crashed over him, and he took a second step back.

Rafi picked up the cup of coffee and took a sip, buying himself time. But the coffee was cold, and Rafi's face collapsed into distaste.

Étienne took the cup from him and tasted the coffee. "It's tepid."

"I like hot things hot and cold things cold." The way he liked knowing what things were about, what was coming next, no surprises or sudden redirection. This whole situation with Étienne was one, big sudden shift and Rafi needed a moment to shift with it.

"I'll warm it up."

"It's okay."

Étienne's voice was gentle and so painfully sweet. "Your overthinking has returned."

Rafi looked up, holding his gaze, instantly regretting it because Étienne's face made any other decision besides staying a near impossibility. "I have errands to run with my father."

"And this?" Étienne asked, taking Rafi's hands in his, while Étienne's eyes held him with quiet insistence. "Will we return to playing basketball and planning parties?"

Panic flared. Rafi pulled his hands away, already regretting being here, regretting leaving, unable to untangle all the feelings that snarled in his chest. "I need time. It's how I'm made."

Étienne dropped his hands, taking an audibly deep breath. "If you'd like to clean up, you can use my bathroom."

Rafi wanted to clear out, but he also smelled...
well, like them. The kind of smell he had to wash
off, because reveling in the memory of the night before would make him change his mind. And he was
already teetering on the edge of staying.

Étienne took a sip of the coffee, savoring it in his
typical, exaggerated fashion. "You're right. Coffee
should be hot." He pointed at a door in the hallway.
"There are extra towels in that closet. Take what
you need."

"Thanks."

Rafi turned away but Étienne took his hand, ar-
resting his escape. Without warning, he pulled Rafi
close and gave him a kiss that had him questioning
every decision he'd ever made. And Rafi melted into
it without thought or protest. Everything he experienced with Étienne ran visceral and deep, especially
this, kissing like he never wanted to stop. It was so
easy to disappear into Étienne. Lose control. Rafi
needed to resist until he could figure out what all
this meant, put himself back together again. When
Étienne pulled away, he turned and sought out the
much-needed escape of a long, hot shower.

Chapter Eighteen

Étienne

Étienne watched Rafi walk away, resisting the urge to follow and persuade him with his hands and body to stay.

He wanted to climb into the shower with Rafi, stroke soapy circles over his skin, watch water shimmer over his compact body and get lost in the whorls of wet curls on his chest and tangles of droplets in his hair. He wanted to take Rafi apart again.

But he couldn't do that, and it stung, brought back that summer night when Rafi ran away, and all the nights after when he remained resolutely unmoved by any overture on Étienne's part.

The door buzzer jolted him out of his thoughts. He couldn't imagine who might be visiting at that time of the morning before he realized the morning had turned to early afternoon.

He answered the buzzer and the last voice he needed to hear came through.

"Philip?"

"It's me. Can I come up?"

His usual excitement at seeing his best friend turned to anxiety. Having Rafi in his flat was not extraordinary. It was Philip and Val's idea that they work together on best-man duties. But this wasn't planning. Étienne was half-dressed, Rafi was showering and there was no mistaking what they'd been up to.

"Still standing here," Philip said.

Étienne pressed the buzzer. "Sorry, come up."

He raced to his room, threw on a shirt and rapped on the bathroom door. It opened, a cloud of vapor billowing out from behind Rafi, clad only in a towel tied low around his waist. Étienne's eyes tracked the droplets of water sprinkled over Rafi's shoulders and imagined licking them off his skin.

This wasn't the time.

"Philip's coming up."

Dazed, Rafi answered, "Oh," before shaking himself out of his stupor. "I won't come out naked if that's what you're worried about."

"You're naked now." And Étienne's hands itched to touch him.

"You know what I mean. Anyway, just best-man stuff, right?" He dug between blankets and pillows, searching for his far-flung clothes. His towel slipped off, doing nothing to improve Étienne's concentration.

"Y-yes," Étienne stammered. "N-nothing to be concerned about."

Rafi pulled his sweater over his head. "We'll play it cool."

Étienne pointed at Rafi's wet hair. "And that?"

Rafi pulled his beanie out of the pocket of his discarded jeans. "Got it covered."

Étienne opened his mouth, poised to speak, but the doorbell rang.

"Okay. Come out when you are ready."

Étienne hurried out of the bedroom to the front door and swung it open, a burst of wind that had trailed in from the cold slamming him in the chest. "Frater!"

"Étienne." Philip stepped inside, shrugging off his coat and shoes. "Don't you answer your phone anymore?"

Étienne had last used it at dinner the night before, but, distracted by Rafi, had abandoned it somewhere he could not immediately recall. "I apologize. Are you okay?"

"We're watching the game this afternoon, remember?" Philip glanced around the apartment. "Do you have company?"

Glancing toward his bedroom, Étienne decided it was best to control the situation before Philip made any deductions of his own. Étienne had no idea how to describe what was happening between him and Rafi to his best friend. "Yes," he answered quickly. "Rafi came over to plan the bachelor party."

Philip grinned. "A party? For moi? What a surprise. Where is he?"

"Bathroom." Étienne pointed toward the kitchen, hoping to redirect Philip's attention. "Sit. I see you staring at my coffee machine."

"Thought I was going to have to beg." Philip folded his long body onto a decorated barstool Étienne had bought and randomly shoved into the corner of his kitchen. Philip always chose it, possibly because it more comfortably accommodated his long legs. "How has it been going with, how is it you called him? A gremlin? Incapable of a surprising act.'"

It seemed like an eon since he'd said those things. "We've gotten past all that."

"That's good," Philip continued, rubbing his chin thoughtfully. "Val was hoping you would find a friend in him."

"A friend in whom?" Rafi said, looking a bit stiff as he did his best imitation of a careless saunter.

"I was just talking about you. Val said you would get along and she was right."

"Uh, yeah, we're cool." Rafi leaned against the doorjamb, eyes fixed on Étienne. Something in his expression left Étienne uneasy. Étienne hoped he did not regret last night, and would decide to leave and contrive some way to avoid Étienne again. It would land harder now Étienne had had a taste of him.

Étienne gave Rafi a quizzical look that he pointedly ignored. "Enjoy the coffee," Rafi added.

"You're not staying?" Philip asked.

"I've been here a while. Practically dragged him out of bed." Rafi clapped Étienne on the back like one of his basketball buddies. "I'll send you that stuff we talked about."

Étienne stared at Rafi's back, fuming irrationally. What had he expected? A kiss goodbye? A seductive "see you tonight, baby"?

"I'll walk you out." Étienne set a mug down in front of Philip and followed Rafi to the door.

"Are you okay?" Étienne whispered when they were in the foyer.

Rafi slipped his socked feet into his black ankle boots and whispered back, "Who, me? Yeah. Great."

"Why do I sense…?"

"You sense nothing. Now go, before Philip gets suspicious." He yanked at the laces of his boots until Étienne thought he might have cut off all circulation to his toes.

"You are confusing."

Rafi stood to his full height. "Gremlins tend to get that way."

"Wait a minute…"

Rafi raised his voice. "Don't tell Philip what we're up to, okay. It's a surprise."

"I love surprises," Philip called back from the kitchen.

Étienne growled as he yanked open the door. "Rafael Navarro." His voice dripped in impotent warning.

"Étienne Galois." Rafi adjusted the beanie to cover his ears and left without another word, leaving Étienne standing in the hallway like a fool.

Étienne returned to the kitchen, where Philip recited the details of the basketball game, a fact that had been swallowed up by everything happening with Rafi lately. He could not go after Rafi the way he wanted to. Scrubbing his face, he turned his attention to Philip, guilty that something as effortless as Philip's company was costing him every ounce of energy.

"I can't tell you what these last couple of months have been like," Philip began.

"Oh, I might have some idea," Étienne sighed.

Philip frowned but pushed on. Val, who had been working with his mother on wedding prep, found herself overwhelmed by the vision the older woman had for her son's wedding. Now Val was working with Sylvana, Étienne's friend, but he'd had to let his mother down carefully, remind her that it was his wedding, not Grace Wagner's Spring Ball they were planning. It had surely stung, not being able to coordinate her only son's nuptials, but with coaxing and lots of conversations with Val, she finally took it in stride.

"But all this wedding prep has left us both exhausted. I'd elope if Val didn't want a wedding so badly."

"You would regret not having a wedding," Étienne said. "Life is short, but it can become long and monotonous if we don't stop to celebrate the milestones along the way."

"You're always so wise." Philip handed Étienne his mug for a refill.

"Easy to be wise about other people's business."

Étienne wanted to unburden himself with Philip about this new and precarious thing with Rafi, the way he'd always done, but he couldn't. Not until

Étienne knew what they were to each other, or if they could even be something to each other.

They spent the rest of the afternoon watching the game and ordered sushi for a late lunch. Rafi didn't text to tell him he'd returned safely, which annoyed Étienne endlessly. Such a little thing to set a mind at ease. But he could do nothing to remedy that. It seemed like both he and Rafi had things to say and it was a game of who would speak first.

Étienne detested those kinds of games.

When Philip finally left, Étienne got dressed as if arming himself for battle. Rafi might be busy or behaving obstinately—with him, there was no way of knowing—but he would not confront either possibility in sweats and house slippers. Sighing soul-deep, he texted Rafi.

Did you arrive home?

Seconds ticked off ad infinitum, wearing on Étienne's nerves. He bundled himself in preparation for a walk, though it was dark and the weather was biting. He closed the apartment door behind him and bounded down the stairs, the vibration of his phone reaching him just as he cleared the outside steps.

Yes.

Étienne walked down the sidewalk, avoiding collisions with other pedestrians. Is that all I get?

Gremlins aren't very talkative.

Étienne bit the inside of his cheek. Offense. Better than rejection. Is that what is troubling you?

I've called you worse.

Étienne sighed. Can I call you?

Arriving at a crosswalk, Étienne was surprised when Rafi's contact appeared on his phone. He stepped into a doorway to take the call.

"You cannot be angry at me," Étienne began.

"I can be any way I want." The sound of clinking glasses and running water meant Rafi was in his apartment.

"But it does not make it fair. You called me an arrogant, devil-may-care flake the night I said that to Philip."

"And as I recall, you told me I was judgmental and rigid."

"I did."

A pause. "Do you still think those things? About me?"

"No, I don't. Do you still think those things about me?"

Rafi sighed, a sound like surrender. "No, I don't think you are a complete devil-may-care flake. Still up in the air about the arrogant part."

"Never a clean win with you."

"What fun would that be?"

Étienne relaxed a bit, though he had one more

doubt to dispel. "And last night? Do you have regrets?"

Rafi paused, but only for a moment. "Last night was…amazing." A pause, then, "Things could get messy."

"I know," Étienne said, relieved that Rafi was giving him a glimpse of his insecurities. "But there is something here. Something worth exploring."

Rafi lapsed into another one of his thoughtful silences, then said, "It feels like everyone has been playing matchmaker since day one."

This took Étienne by surprise. "Val, as well?"

"Especially Val. She's the captain of this ship."

Étienne leaned against the building, away from a gust of cold wind. He almost wanted to ask what the trouble was. Why was Rafi fighting this so hard? But it wasn't a complete mystery. "If that's the case, we should not disappoint her."

Étienne could almost hear the clanging of Rafi's overthinking. "What do you mean?"

He might regret his next words, but he would regret it more if he let Rafi slip away without saying them. "I want to see you again."

Rafi fell quiet again and Étienne waited. He was beginning to learn that Rafi needed time to process things.

"We have a wedding to help pull off," Rafi finally said.

"Yes, we do," Étienne said carefully. "But I don't mean only the wedding."

Rafi's breath had gone ragged. "I gathered that."

Long moments crawled by in which Étienne expected Rafi to say something to put an end to this, and with good reason. Getting mixed up with Rafi was a terrible idea, but one night together had made him reckless.

"Let's start with planning and go from there."

"Is that what we're calling it?"

"I just want to be careful. I'm not good at…being impulsive."

"You don't have to be. I can be impulsive enough for the both of us."

A soft huff of laughter came through the phone. "Next weekend?"

Étienne wanted to punch the air. "Same time, same place."

"It's a…well, it's a date." Rafi cleared his throat. "I should get going. Val's waiting for me at her place."

"And off you go to save her." A gust of wind reminded Étienne he was still standing outside. The cold was getting to him despite his coat, but he was glowing from the promise of seeing Rafi again.

"She does a fair amount of rescuing, too, when I need it."

"I have no doubts." Étienne's voice was starting to shiver. "I should find somewhere to warm up."

"You were outside this whole time?" Rafi's voice changed, grew commanding. And Étienne liked it. "All you need is to catch a cold. Go inside."

"Yes, sir," Étienne practically purred because oh, how he liked the sound of that.

"I'm hanging up."

He raised the collar of his coat and started moving back in the direction of his apartment. He'd had enough of this damned cold. "Not without saying good night. I will call again if you don't."

"You're impossible," Rafi snapped, and Étienne took delight at the return of his ornery temper. "Good night, then."

"Bon nwi, cherie."

Étienne needed a moment to get his bearings after they ended their call. He buzzed with the excitement of seeing more of Rafi. It might be a mistake, and no matter Val and the family's enthusiasm, this was not to be taken lightly. But Étienne had never shied away from reaching for the fruit this life had to offer. Not after it had taken so much from him.

And Rafi was the sweetest fruit of all.

Chapter Nineteen

Rafi

Étienne's *"Bon nwi, cherie"* rang in Rafi's head for days after they'd spoken. To be fair, with the amount of chemistry between them, it was only a matter of time before something sparked and exploded. Rafi had simply pulled the pin without letting go of the grenade.

Rafi scrubbed his face, resting his elbows on his kitchen counter. "But it was good," he muttered to himself. And that made not thinking about Étienne ten thousand times harder. In the week leading up to their next meeting, he tried distracting himself with work, his family, the endless minutae of wedding planning that he'd agreed to help Val with. And each time, he was plagued with thoughts of Étienne.

He knew better than to get mixed up with some-one like Étienne. He should say no, cut him off be-fore Rafi did anything more with him and they both ended up with a pile of regrets. Étienne was too much and Rafi had already learned his lesson about the consequences of losing control, and making stupid decisions. He had a long history of them, romantic and otherwise.

And yet, the weekend couldn't come soon enough.

Rafi barely heard the knock on the door above the roar of his hair dryer. Normally, people who wanted to see him rang from the outside. Only his family had access to his interior door. When he swung it open, shivering in his T-shirt, and still damp from his shower, he fully expected his father to be on the other side. Étienne, framed in his doorway, impec-cable dark coat dusted with melting snow and hold-ing a plastic bag with aluminium containers inside, was beyond his expectation.

Rafi's brain had trouble computing Étienne's presence. He let entire seconds tick by before his thoughts came back online again and he remembered that words were still an option.

"Uh…hi." Rafi even waved at him, his breath coming in as if he'd sprinted up a flight of stairs. "What are you doing here?"

Étienne grinned, holding up the plastic bag. "Val had roasted goat on the menu."

Rafi gasped out a laugh that surged from unex-pected emotion. It flooded him from head to toe as the reality of Étienne sharpened before him. "That's a lot of roasted goat."

"It is," Étienne retorted. He surprised Rafi by bending down to leave a kiss on his cheek, making him forget the cold. "But I could be persuaded to share. Have you eaten?"

Rafi went a little lightheaded at the way Étienne's voice dropped low near his ear. "Not yet. It's a little early for me." He shook the sensation away. "You didn't message me. What if I hadn't been home?"

Étienne pulled back, the expression in those dark eyes making Rafi's stomach swoop. "Then I would have left. But it was a risk worth taking."

Rafi stepped aside. "I guess if you're already here, come in."

Étienne gave him another massive grin as he stepped past him, carrying with him the crisp aroma of a frozen late afternoon, laundered clothes and the slight musk of man hidden under it all. Rafi's mouth watered at the thought of Étienne bending to give him one of those kisses that made him melt like candlewax. "Hang up your coat. I'll put this in the oven to keep warm."

Étienne did as he was told with impressive obedience while Rafi escaped into the kitchen just beyond his tiny living room.

Some gray light from the frigid sunset filtered in from the high, rectangular windows of his apartment, illuminating the interior with muted light. Rafi took in his apartment through Étienne's eyes, immediately noting the contrast between their respective spaces. Rafi's decor was linear and immaculate, metallic grays and blues characterizing the overall color scheme. Marble counters and ultramodern furniture screamed Single Man Abhors Dirt. Much more monochromatic than Étienne's color explosion. Rafi felt remarkably vulnerable, as if something fundamental was being revealed by his choice of throw pillows. Relief flooded him when Étienne joined him in the kitchen.

"The weather is garbage," Rafi said as he warmed the oven.

"Ah, the weather," Étienne mused. "The tried-and-true conversation starter."

"You have a better topic?" Rafi retorted.

"Perhaps something like 'did you miss me?'"

Rafi made a face. "We spoke yesterday about your best-man gift, remember?"

"Not the same at all."

Rafi gave him in exaggerated sigh, a fizzy sense of happiness threatening to swallow him up. "Fine. Did you miss me?"

"Not at all."

Rafi punched Étienne lightly on the shoulder, his fist finding unyielding, fabric-wrapped muscle. Étienne was wearing a tan Henley that looked tailor-made for the sable-brown wool trousers he wore. "I didn't miss you, either."

Étienne's smile burned with smug victory, which annoyed Rafi but also thrilled him. "What do you have to drink?"

Rafi winced at his lack of manners and opened

his refrigerator, examining the meager options inside. "Beer? Wine? A suspicious-looking carton of orange juice?"

"Beer is good, if it's not expired," Étienne quipped, taking a seat at the kitchen counter. Étienne's eyes fell to the floor, with its exposed concrete and patches of dried hot glue from the previous floor covering. "This is what Caio was talking about when he mentioned he would be redoing your floors."

Rafi scowled at the thought of Caio having any kind of conversation alone with Étienne, even though Rafi loved him dearly. "You got a lot of information from such a short conversation." He put the containers of food inside the oven. When he turned, he found himself nose-to-nose with Étienne.

"Does it bother you?"

Rafi opened his mouth, then closed it, managing to get another nose full of Étienne, which sent his system into overload. "No," he croaked out.

Étienne chuckled, disbelief written across his face, then took a seat opposite Rafi. Rafi couldn't keep his eyes off him as he set out two bottles of beer and two glasses before sinking into his own chair. "I didn't think I'd see you again until the weekend," Rafi blurted out.

The mischief drained from Étienne's face. "I'm not good at waiting."

"Impatient and incapable of keeping an appointment," Rafi said, unraveling even as he teased him. "Got it."

Étienne's hand found Rafi's across the table. "I'm easier to figure out than most."

Fingers threaded together, Étienne's thumb rubbed circles over Rafi's and it was the best sensation Rafi had experienced since the last time Étienne had touched him. Rafi's control was growing tenuous again, giddiness replacing caution and fear, and he wanted to shake himself out of it, but couldn't. Couldn't look away from Étienne's lips, the softness that waited there for him.

"I brainstormed a few more ideas for the bachelor party," Rafi said, in a desperate, last measure to cool them both down.

"Did you?" Étienne answered, fingers still working some kind of magic on Rafi's skin. "Funny, the only thing I could think about was you."

Rafi's skin grew tight, unbearable. It was the height of irresponsibility to not use this precious time with Étienne to do some planning, but further thoughts got lost in the rapid rise and fall of Étienne's breathing. Rafi's own heart felt like it would split in two from too much beating. He glanced at the unopened bottles between them, the quiet expectation that they would be emptied clashing with Rafi's certainty that they would not. He dragged his eyes back to Étienne's, which were heavy and dark, and he felt the fabric of his control shred and give way.

Rafi leaned in, holding Étienne's gaze until his vision doubled and he was forced to close his eyes. He could tell himself in fifty different ways what a bad idea this was, but it was a bad idea he desperately needed, desire for Étienne pulsing all the way down to his bones. Étienne's lips were whisper-soft against Rafi's, sculpted to fit his. He bit gently down on the plump flesh, drawing a tiny moan from Étienne, before soothing it with his tongue. Rafi could get obsessed with this man and that feet-off-the-ground sensation had him clawing for more.

Étienne pulled back to catch his breath, pressing his forehead to Rafi's. "I showed you mine, now show me yours."

"You've seen… I thought… Haven't you?" Rafi stammered.

"I meant," Étienne said between kissing Rafi's knuckles, tiny droplets of sensation raining over his skin, "show me your bedroom."

They had a to-do list the size of Rafi's arm. There were other conversations to be had, other plans to be made. And this was *Étienne*, for goodness sake. Coming and going and doing without a care for consequences. But the taste of reckless want that Étienne inspired flooded his mouth, made him ache and he took him back to his bedroom. It was only fair, and Rafi was nothing if not fair.

Chapter Twenty

Étienne

The room was as diminutive as the rest of Rafi's apartment but managed to be warmer despite the matching cool tones. Perhaps it was the giant pillows across the blue, padded headboard, the plush, down comforters that made the colors positively pulse with the promise of heat. Or maybe it was the way Étienne imagined Rafi across those covers as Étienne did all the things that had him in a fever dream of heat these last few days.

Rafi had not untangled their fingers, even when he tilted his head to press his lips to Étienne's. Rafi made to pull away but Étienne stilled his retreat with a hand on the back of his head.

"You're very sweet, you know that?" Étienne said.

Rafi frowned, though his cheeks flushed pink. "I've never been called sweet before."

"You are," Étienne said, threading his fingers through Rafi's soft brown curls, which Rafi leaned into. "Not all the way through. More like something tart with a lingering after taste."

"You just described me as sour candy."

Étienne laughed, stroking Rafi's scalp. "You're impossible to flirt with. How did I get you into bed the first time?"

Rafi's hand came up around Étienne's neck, surprising him with his strength as he pulled Étienne to within an inch of his face. "You finally shut up so I could kiss you."

Étienne emptied his laughter into Rafi's mouth, which opened to allow him inside. This was Étienne's weakness—kissing Rafi until he had no other useful thought in his head. Rafi's hands slid under his sweater, the drag of his warm palms scorching a path along Étienne's stomach until Rafi tucked them under the waist of his beltless pants. The grunt Étienne gave was indecent, but Rafi was kryptonite for his self-control.

"You're overdressed," Rafi murmured into Étienne's shoulder.

"So are you," he retorted, flipping Rafi's T-shirt over his head and shoving down his sweatpants, then hissing at the realization that Rafi wore nothing underneath.

"Were you hoping I would visit?" Étienne growled

as Rafi dropped onto the mattress, scrabbling backward until he reached the middle.

"Bold of you to assume that I was waiting for you," he said, stroking himself as he watched Étienne's ever more frenzied efforts to get his own clothes off. "Maybe I had other plans before you showed up."

Every filthy Creole curse word Étienne had ever known fell from his lips as he kneeled onto the mattress. He wanted to be the only thing on Rafi's list, the only plan he ever made.

"You'll pay for that," Étienne warned, sinking his entire weight onto Rafi, pinning him. His kisses grew harder as he ground his hips into Rafi's, the stroke of their erections sending shivers of electricity up and down Étienne's spine. Their kisses grew more frantic as a flush of heat and exertion spread over Rafi's skin. Étienne buried his nose in Rafi's neck, taking in his scent.

"You smell good enough to eat," Étienne said, reveling in the salt and heat of Rafi's skin.

Rafi shifted, sliding his legs open to cradle Étienne's hips in his. "Do it already." He pulled him down for a long kiss.

Étienne palmed him roughly before he leaned back on his haunches, searching for his pants. Rafi hissed and reached up in retaliation, tweaking Étienne's oversensitive nipples before flicking his chin toward the end table. "Everything you need is there."

Étienne rummaged inside the drawer, finding

lube and condoms. He slicked his fingers and, nibbling with blunt teeth on Rafi's nipples, worked him slowly, easing his fingers inside becoming familiar with the ways Rafi's body reacted to his touch, the strokes and touches that pulled those small, unselfconscious sounds he loved to hear. The reserved Rafi that slayed him with his hesitancies and awkward pauses was gone. Rafi moved against Étienne's fingers, unselfconscious as he searched without shame for his pleasure.

"Are you ready?" Étienne whispered against his ear.

Rafi nodded, helping Étienne smooth his condom on. Étienne bit his lip and slowly pressed into Rafi, his body seizing with the shock of intimacy, of being so close, they breathed each other in. The warm weight of Rafi's legs was wound tight around Étienne's body as his hips surged. Rafi's raw groan told Étienne he'd hit that sweet spot that made fireworks go off in Rafi's body and Étienne went after Rafi's pleasure with unerring precision.

Dangerous thoughts pressed at Étienne—how he wanted, more than anything, for Rafi to recognize him as the architect of his pleasure, wanted to be the first and last person who got to put his hands on Rafi each day. That the idea of him finding this with anyone else but Étienne made him want to claw and crush with his bare hands.

He bit the words back before they incriminated him and redoubled his efforts. Rafi had his hands flung over his head, finding purchase by holding on to the edge of the mattress, and arched into Étienne. Sweat glittered over his olive skin and Étienne wanted to lick each muscle as it bunched and swelled with tension. Lips curled, teeth gritted, he held on as Étienne rocked into him. Rafi came that way, his body bowed, his own spend arching across his stomach without having touched himself and it was more than Étienne could bear. He rode Rafi through his orgasm and focused on his own pleasure, jerking his hips as he came soon after, shuddering against a shivering Rafi, his vision whiting out at the edges.

When Étienne came back to himself, he had tucked his head into the crook of Rafi's neck, Rafi's nails scraping his tight curls, warm and solid as a palm tree on the beach, a place for Étienne to moor himself in the whirlwind of his existence. Étienne was past the territory of want and desire, rapidly heading into the treacherous terrain of need. And he couldn't stop himself from falling into it full-throttle, without brakes to slow him down.

Étienne didn't know how to say all these things without overwhelming Rafi with his feelings and perhaps scaring him into retreat. He simply sighed and said, "You feel good."

Rafi's chuckle rumbled in Étienne's ear. "What will you tell Val about her goat this time?"

"Hmm," Étienne said, shifting, feeling all the decadent aches and discomforts of a round of good sex. "I'll tell her it was the best I've ever had." Étienne lifted his head to look at Rafi, who looked thoroughly blissed out. "There is something to be said for not planning every last eventuality."

"You must think I'm the most boring person on Earth," Rafi said quietly.

Étienne pulled back, resting his weight on his elbow instead of Rafi's warm chest. "Where did you get that idea?"

Rafi shrugged. "I mean, it wouldn't be the first time someone has said that."

Étienne was starting to feel a murderous urge rise up in him. "Who would say such a thing? And where can I find him?"

Rafi laughed, pulling Étienne roughly down to hug him to his chest. "Knowing you, Mr. Zero Impulse Control, you probably would go find him." Étienne growled, unamused. "It's nobody who matters now. I would just hate it if you, of all people, thought that way."

"I don't think that way. I like the way you are. I like that you are solid and dependable and somewhat dogmatic." Rafi frowned at the last part. "I only mean that you have a very fixed idea of things and that is not necessarily a bad thing. In fact to me—" Étienne swallowed *"—ou pafé."*

Rafi barked out a laugh. "Perfect? Yeah, says the globe-trotting photographer who speaks five languages, looks like a model and makes love like a demon."

Étienne grabbed Rafi's chin and held it firmly in place. "Says the man who hasn't had a person to call his own outside of his family in a very long time. I can run to the ends of the earth, but each corner looks the same when you don't have a heart to come back to."

Rafi swallowed hard, the smooth column of his neck rippling rhythmically. "I'm the farthest thing from perfect in the world." Rafi slid out from under Étienne and rolled onto his side, forcing Étienne to drop his hand.

"Rafi?"

Étienne's view of Rafi's torso—a perfect triangle with defined shoulders that tapered to a narrow waist—was all he could see of him, as his face was hidden.

"You know I got into this fight once. I was fourteen." Rafi's back rose and fell with his sigh. "I was just figuring out how to be myself. It helped that there was a group of us queer kids who gravitated toward each other and looked out for one another. You met some of them."

Étienne made an encouraging sound, letting Rafi speak.

"This kid was a jerk. He called me a name, so I punched him in the mouth."

"Sounds like he earned it."

Rafi's sigh was more pronounced this time and Étienne almost feared he might have misspoken. "They called the restaurant—everybody knew I was Enrique and Gabriela's kid. Said my parents had to come up to the school and get me. The restaurant was slow and Mami's English was always better than Papi's, so she decided to pick me up." A shiver rippled through Rafi's body. Étienne wanted desperately to touch him, smooth out whatever pained him. But something told him to wait.

"She left the restaurant, but she never made it to the school. A motorcycle clipped her as she was walking. She hit her head, lost consciousness and never woke up again."

Now the urge to hold Rafi overwhelmed Étienne's good sense. Étienne wrapped himself around Rafi like a duvet, cocooning him in all the warmth he could muster. To Étienne's relief, Rafi accepted this and, instead of resisting, pressed his back against Étienne's chest.

"Why are you telling me this now?" Étienne whispered.

Rafi shrugged. "I'm not perfect, that's all. That experience changed all of us…me." He looked over his shoulder to better observe Étienne. The hollow expression crushed Étienne and he squeezed him tighter. "Maybe not for the better. And you should know that before you…get more involved."

Étienne frowned. "With all due respect, Rafi. My family survived an earthquake. Does that diminish us in any way?"

Rafi's eyes grew wide. "No, of course not. But it's not the same." His eyes slid away. "It wasn't your fault."

"It is very much the same. Something terrible happened to us that was beyond both our control." Rafi shook his head but Etienne pushed on. "It may have changed who we were meant to be, but that doesn't make us less." Étienne took Rafi's hand and kissed his wrist, Rafi's heartbeat fluttering against his lips.

"I'm just trying to be transparent," Rafi said.

"I appreciate that, but I must respectfully disagree with you."

Rafi's lips quirked into a half smile. "Duly noted." There were still clouds in his expression, but something in the rosy tint of his skin and the glint of his eyes said he'd liked Étienne's words. "I wasn't lying about the bachelor party. I actually do have a few ideas to share with you."

Étienne shifted, finally feeling the mess they made. "We can clean up and discuss it over your sister's goat, yes?"

Rafi settled in closer to his side, tucking himself in, which struck at a tender place in Étienne's chest. "Okay. But can we just stay like this a few more minutes?"

"Yes," he said quietly, allowing Rafi to press into Étienne and find whatever comfort he seemed to need.

Chapter Twenty-One

Rafi

Back-breaking sex notwithstanding, the search for Philip's bachelor-party venue was not immediately successful. Every place he and Étienne visited fell short of their expectations, which Rafi was beginning to think were a bit high. He could ask Val for ideas but the deeper she got into her own planning, the more stressed out she got, and anyway, he preferred solving these things with Étienne, who was more resourceful than Rafi anticipated. And more fun. Definitely more fun.

Getting around the snow-bound city was endlessly annoying, but the upside was that no matter how cold or snowy it got, they always returned to Étienne's flat to warm each other up, far away from the very demands that brought them together, though Papi had commented more than once on Rafi's newfound penchant for disappearing over the weekend.

But with deadlines for bookings approaching and Étienne's next business trip looming ever closer, timing was becoming critical, and they still hadn't found what they were looking for.

"I have a professional acquaintance," Étienne said when Rafi called him after another round of dissatisfying searching. Rafi had been avoiding leaving his classroom to face the snowdrifts that had piled up on either side of the sidewalk. He worked hard to ignore the way the lilt of Étienne's words and the tangle of vowels in his mouth rolled through him. "He owns a hotel downtown. It would not have been my first choice because the location is not perfect for the locales you identified, but it does have an indoor, heated pool and splendid suites. A change in itinerary would still make it feasible."

It almost sounded reasonable. "Let's check it out."

"I can pick you up," Étienne said.

"You sure? I can meet you…"

"Absolutely not. Snow is expected again this weekend. I will make the arrangements."

Rafi was feeling a little breathless. "Okay."

"Do you know what I will do when I…come to you?" Étienne whispered.

"I have a few ideas." Rafi's voice went shaky. He glanced at the classroom door, hoping no one knocked because he couldn't stand up, even if the building had been on fire.

"You don't. You can't imagine all the ways I will debauch you."

Rafi gripped his phone like a lifeline to reality. *Debauch?* Was this Rafi's life? "I'd probably…let you."

Rafi was really bringing the sexy.

Étienne's husky laugh pulled Rafi's body taut and he groaned, "I'm not… I'm not as good with words as you are."

"I would disagree. In the proper context, you say all the right things. I especially like it when you say *please.*"

Rafi's mouth had gone dry. "I have to go… I'm at work."

"Wait for this weekend and I will give you relief."

"That made nothing better."

Rafi ended the call, and dropped the phone, holding his head in his hands. A few more words and he would have come at his work desk. Étienne could unhinge him, turn him into a plaything with only a few words. Rafi picked up a stack of papers and alphabetized them by the last name of each student, the lull of repetitive work driving the pulse of desire down to a manageable rhythm. But it was always in the background, a replay on loop—the way Étienne kissed him, the sound of his words in his ear, the burning ache when he took him in his mouth.

The papers slipped out of his hand and scattered over his desk and onto the floor.

Rafi tugged at his hair, the sharp pain bringing him back to the present before he dropped to his knees—he wanted that, too, dammit—and gathered his papers with shaky hands.

* * *

"This could work." Rafi had his tablet open with a map he'd created to mark out all the places to visit during the barhop. He and Étienne were sitting in the lobby of the hotel where they'd completed a tour of the facilities, including the glass-enclosed heated pool, which made Rafi feel as if they were caught in an inverted snow globe, where white flakes swirled beyond the glass, not inside. A lull in the falling drifts had convinced them it was possible to keep their appointment, though the sky was limned in silver, pregnant with the promise of more snow.

Étienne took the chair next to Rafi, leaning in with the pretext of studying the computer screen. Rafi angled it so Étienne could get a better view, but craved the contact, despite the way it disrupted his train of thought. Étienne pointed his long, solid forefinger at each location and said something that Rafi had to ask him to repeat.

"The restaurant we originally had our heart set on is too far out of the way. However, this one is well-reviewed."

"So cocktails at the hotel bar, dinner here and then…" Rafi traced with his finger the trajectory of each stop, which, demon that Étienne was, he captured by hooking his own around Rafi's.

"Behave," Rafi ordered with his sternest voice.

Étienne turned to him, eyes smoldering and flicking to his lips before capturing his gaze again. "Make. Me."

"We're in public," Rafi said in a whisper-shout,

though the smile that threatened to break away diluted his tone.

"Later, then." Étienne relaxed into his chair, grinning. "I am impressed. You had a plan and with minimal angst, you were able to change it and embrace a new one."

Rafi shut his computer and packed everything in his case. "I don't have a problem changing plans when presented with new information. What I can't handle is not having a plan at all. I'm not good at thinking on my feet the way you are."

"Is that a compliment?" Étienne leaned forward, his face close to Rafi's.

Rafi's skin flushed uncontrollably hot. "It's why we're a good team."

Étienne's face softened, all humor gone, replaced with something more ardent. He used his forefinger to give Rafi's knee one short, gentle stroke. "I like to think so, too."

It was more than good teamwork. All Rafi's overthinking did not diminish the fact that Rafi wanted Étienne all the time. But he had no plan for Étienne, no endgame. He couldn't see where this would lead and the uncertainty of it made Rafi dizzy.

The only feeling more disorienting than this uncertainty was the one that suffused him each time he thought of Étienne's hands on him.

As Étienne made all the arrangements with his contact, Rafi's phone lit up with a weather alert. It confirmed what forecasters had been warning for days—another storm was coming through. He worried about the roads—it was more snow than they usually got during this time of the year.

Étienne returned from his conversation, "It's all booked. It will be a matter of a few calls to organize the remainder of the evening."

"Which is my part of it. But we should get going so we can beat the snow. Let's go to my place. It's closer."

Étienne frowned. "But what about your family…"

"Val's home with Philip and Nati's at the hospital all weekend. It's Papi. I'd rather not leave him alone in this." Rafi drew close, despite his admonishment about being in the lobby of the hotel, in full view of whoever passed. "Papi never comes down to my place." Rafi placed a hand on Étienne's hip beneath his coat, squeezing gently. "Anyway, you haven't been by since I put in my new floors."

Étienne's face split into a wide grin. "An unconventional method of seduction."

Rafi wanted to bury his nose in the soft spot under Étienne's ear. "They're the sexiest floors you've ever seen."

"How can I resist?"

The drive to Rafi's apartment was less difficult than he thought, but by the time they reached Navarro's, the sky had cracked open like eggshells, blanketing even the pretreated sidewalks in a sea of white.

Rafi and Étienne pounded the snow from their boots on the mat outside Rafi's apartment, brushing it from their coats and hanging everything on hooks before racing inside despite the heating elements in the hallway going overtime. Rafi barely had a chance to shake out the tangle of curls he'd released from his beanie when he was in Étienne's arms, swallowed by his bulk, his lips, the unrelenting heat of his body. And Rafi dissolved into him like the snow turning to puddles on his doorstep. Rafi broke away, breathless, his logical brain trying, in vain, to put into sequence any two thoughts that did not involve Étienne.

"So?" Rafi gasped.

"*So* what?" Étienne murmured from the spot on his neck where his lips grazed.

Rafi pulled back. "What do you think of my floors?"

Étienne blinked rapidly, looking dazedly around himself. "I am slayed by them."

Rafi grabbed the buckle of Étienne's belt and undid it. "Somehow, I don't think you're appreciating them the way they deserved to be appreciated."

Étienne's eyes flashed, dark and bottomless with promise. He pulled off Rafi's sweater and unbuttoned his shirt with a speed that left Rafi dizzy. "I will appreciate them, in painstaking detail—" he palmed Rafi's erection through his jeans and that blew out several million nerve endings from that touch alone "—after."

Chapter Twenty-Two

Rafi

Rafi woke to an annoying shaft of sunlight streaming in through the windows set high in the bedroom, announcing the snowstorm had come to an end sometime the night before. Too busy getting lost in Étienne, he'd abandoned his nightly routines, including pulling the curtains closed, which he always did before going to bed. Hard to have regrets when Étienne looked so irresistible, twisted up in Rafi's duvet, which, incidentally, he'd snatched completely for himself, leaving Rafi with next to nothing. A blanket hog.

It was both messy and charming as hell.

Rafi rubbed his face, which caused Étienne to roll away in his sleep, taking the last scrap of material with him. Rafi rose as gently as he could, stopping only to pull the curtains shut before tiptoeing into the bathroom, careful to switch on only the night-light to tend to his needs. He glanced at himself in the mirror in the dim light, the signs of lovemaking visible on his body, and bit back a smile like an absolute simp.

Étienne was scorching a path through his existence and he was grinning like it was the best thing that had ever happened to him. All that agonizing, fretting and planning, thrown aside for him. Étienne had once said he could be impulsive enough for both of them, but here Rafi was, trashing all the rules he'd set up for himself, as he knew he would, with zero thought to what would come next.

He stepped out of the small space to find Étienne stretching his luxuriously long body. He sat up suddenly, rubbing his eyes.

"You were gone."

Rafi's pinched his lip at the familiar tableau, a mirror of his own reaction to waking in Étienne's place. "My apartment? During a snowstorm? Not likely."

"And here I thought you couldn't stand to leave because of me."

A half smile quirked the edges of Rafi's lips. "That, too."

"I prefer that explanation." Étienne pulled Rafi down next to him and covered them both with the stolen duvet. Étienne ran a hand, firm and possessive, over Rafi's hip and thigh that made Rafi feel like nothing could get to him. Rafi returned the caress, Étienne's skin still warm from sleep and inhaled the irresistible musk of him.

"What's it like to be so hot all the time?" Rafi asked.

Étienne chuckled, bending his head to nuzzle the corners of Rafi's lip before diving in for one long, languid kiss. Rafi could do this all day—kiss Étienne until they were both raw from it.

When Étienne pulled back, he said, "My parents want to invite you to dinner."

Rafi jerked his head back, surprised. "Really?"

Étienne nodded. "They enjoy getting to know my…" He swallowed hard.

Rafi frowned, filling in the rest of his sentence. "Friends?"

Étienne stroked down Rafi's back, sliding over his hip, which he squeezed again. "I would like to think we are more than friends."

Tension wound itself around Rafi's body, squeezing hard. He shook off his stupor and sat up, grabbing a pillow, and hugging it to his chest. "I was hoping to keep things quiet until after the wedding."

Étienne sat up, too. Glorious dark limbs folded one over the other, no effort to cover anything. Why should he? He was magnificent. He took Rafi's hand, twining their fingers together. "What if I want them to know? What if I want to make what we have… official?"

Rafi studied him, not understanding. "Why not wait? The wedding is around the corner."

"It feels like an eternity," Étienne said, reaching for him. "I would like to tell people about us. I don't want to pretend we are just friends."

"But Philip? Aren't you worried about overshadowing his wedding?"

Étienne bit his lip and that flicker of uncertainty was nothing like the confident, brash Étienne he knew. It was unexpected and Rafi could only hold still and wait, unable to anticipate what was coming next.

"Why should it? I understand not wanting to damage relationships we both hold dear if we were to disappoint each other's expectations." He brought Rafi's knuckles to his lips. "But I am not trifling with you. This is not a casual affair for me."

Rafi's breath rattled like chains in his chest, his fingers curling around Étienne in spasms of incoming panic.

"Being with you makes me more certain every day that you are not someone I want only for a week or a month, but for as long as you will have me."

"Étienne…" Rafi felt the beating of his heart as it nearly sputtered to a stop. He gently pulled his hands from Étienne's grasp.

"I can sense…" Étienne said, searching Rafi's face. "I can sense your hesitation."

"It's not… I'm not…" Rafi stammered, but insinuating he had no qualms or doubts was a lie he didn't want to tell. "It feels really sudden. Meeting parents shouldn't be something you do on impulse."

"It's not an impulse. I've thought this through. But

if you're not ready, I understand. I simply needed you to know where I stand."

"I appreciate that," Rafi answered.

Étienne waited, watching him, perhaps expecting him to respond with something thoughtful, something to acknowledge the enormity of what Étienne was saying. But Rafi's mind had gone blank, like an endless expanse of white. He hadn't thought as far ahead as Étienne had. Rafi had been moving from one milestone to the next, without a thought as to what might happen after Val's wedding and their collaboration was at an end. Being caught unawares and without a plan, Rafi was aggressively adrift, awash in uncertainty, and the ever-present fear that came with making a decision without thinking through what would come next.

Étienne grew paler with every moment that passed. "Maybe I've phrased things improperly. I want to introduce you to my parents because I want to go public with our relationship."

"I…" Rafi was genuinely at a loss for words. "I gathered as much." He pushed the pillow aside and searched for his pants, yanking them on blindly.

"I wish you wouldn't do that."

Rafi froze. "Do what?"

"Pull away when things get intense."

"I'm not pulling away. I need time…"

"I'm in love with you, Rafael."

Rafi couldn't breathe. He stared at Étienne, and didn't recognize him, not without the charm or the flourish, the mischievous twist of his lips or the glint of fire in his eyes that was so much a part of who he was. It was Étienne alone, without artifice, deprived of his usual defenses. The purity of him unmoored Rafi. Rafi's control was slipping and if he wasn't careful, he'd fall into this, and then, what would come next? He had no idea. Terror was a poor description for what coursed through him at Étienne's words.

At his lack of response, Étienne got to his feet and began pacing. "Haven't you heard a word I've been saying? I am in love with you, Rafael Navarro. I want to be with you."

Panic thundered through Rafi. Étienne was light and joy, he was joie de vivre in person. What was happening?

"We've only known each other for a few months. I—"

Étienne stiffened. "It was an inelegant way to confess my feelings."

"No, it's—it's okay. I just…"

"Don't feel the same way about me?"

"No… Yes… I…dammit. I—" Rafi stood suddenly, the room reeling as he did. He blinked rapidly and reminded himself to breathe. "I need a minute to think."

Étienne's forehead furrowed, his frown deep as he mirrored Rafi's search for clothing, pulling them on with a speed that terrified Rafi. "Feelings are not subject to logic. You either feel something or you don't."

Rafi's temper flared, anger an easier emotion to handle than the myriad of other feelings poised to break over him. "Not everyone is as clear or easy with seizing the moment as you are. I know I'm not. I need to… I don't know—figure things out."

"Perhaps, for once, allow yourself to simply feel something without overthinking it."

"I'm not built that way," Rafi retorted, hating the turn their conversation was taking.

"No, you're not. And I am a fool who spoke too soon." Étienne yanked his socks on. "Twice the fool for you."

"Are you trying to guilt me?"

"No. I am trying to figure out why I cannot seem to protect myself when it comes to you, why I am always exposing my heart to someone who has never felt the way I do."

"That's unfair."

"Is it?"

Rafi wanted to tell him it wasn't true, that he wasn't alone in his feelings, that Rafi felt something. A lot. But he didn't know what to call it or how to quantify it and if he had a little more time, he might figure it out, but he couldn't throw himself into something like this.

"I need to see the end of things, that's all." Rafi followed him into the living room.

Étienne paused in the gathering of his personal effects, which he'd tossed willy-nilly around Rafi's apartment. "You are seeing the end of things. You are obsessed with outcomes and consequences. Well, here they are."

Étienne pulled the door open, hands shaking as he

pulled his coat off the hook and threw on his winter accessories without method or care.

"It's been snowing all night." Rafi's voice was barely above a whisper. "You can't go home in this."

Étienne stared down at Rafi, his eyes unrelenting in their pain. He hadn't hidden his heart from him, and he refused to hide his hurt, as well. Rafi wanted to say so much, had an endless store of words, but they were crushed under an unyielding mass of disorientation. "If you let me leave, I won't return. I cannot continue to allow you to hurt me this way."

Rafi choked on an answer, like cut glass caught in his throat. He heard Étienne's resentment and knew he deserved so much more than Rafi's paralysis. Here was the confirmation of all of Rafi's fears, the price he would have to pay for giving in to the way he felt for Étienne. He couldn't do what Étienne was asking him to do. "I'm not like you."

Étienne closed his eyes, like a man who'd taken a blow that had tested the limits of his strength, then turned on his heel and strode down the hallway. A bitter draft of cold wind and the singular brightness of bleached snow struck Rafi hard when Étienne pulled the heavy door open. He watched Étienne disappear into it, one blinding light swallowing the other until the door clicked shut, leaving Rafi in the frozen gloom of the hallway, alone.

Chapter Twenty-Three

Étienne

Étienne must have snapped at Alán one too many times because Alán got up, slammed the prints on to the drafting desk and told Étienne exactly where he could shove his camera before storming out of the room.

Étienne ran his hands over his hair, which he'd trimmed haphazardly that morning, with uneven results, and debated going after Alán. He was behaving abominably and had been for weeks. He thought the reprieve of an extended business trip from his day-to-day, post-Rafi life might improve his humor, but Étienne had returned after his trip as miserable as when he'd left. However, it was hardly Alán's fault.

It was up to Étienne to make peace with his assistant, but Étienne was too miserable to do the right thing.

That his mood had nothing to do with anyone within striking distance of where he sat, surrounded by backdrops and reflectors, was irrelevant. He was hurt and angry and unhappy, and the logical part of his brain didn't care about the hows and whys, only that the object of his turmoil was frustratingly out of reach.

To Étienne's surprise, Alán marched back into the room and shoved a bottle of water into Étienne's hand.

"Imbesil," he snapped, switching to Creole. "Drink this before I do something only you will regret."

Étienne took a long drag, the cold water quenching some of his misery. When he had downed the entire bottle, he said, "Only me? What about you?"

"Why would I have regrets about beating you after the way you have been behaving? No regrets." He waved a finger in Étienne's face. "Not. One."

Étienne scrubbed at his beard again. "I'm sorry. I've been a little short-tempered lately."

"A little short-tempered?" Alán exclaimed, holding his hands together as if he were praying for patience. "You've been worse than an angry bear. I have never seen you like this. I don't like this version of you, not at all. You need to go, make up with Rafael and spare us your unhappiness."

Étienne tossed the empty bottle in the recycling basket. "It's not my move to make." He clasped his hands together, bringing them to his forehead, as if he could purge his obsessive thoughts of Rafi with a thump of his fist. Étienne had made the fatal error of exposing himself to Rafi yet again, and yet again, Rafi had made it clear Étienne was not what he wanted.

Étienne thought of Rafi's hesitations, how difficult it was for him to give in to his own emotions, his own pleasure. He was tangled in the convolutions his mind used to justify his fears. Étienne could love him, but he could not alter the workings of his thoughts. "I miscalculated."

"Have you tried speaking to him? You are usually persuasive."

"I shouldn't have to be persuasive about this. I cannot continue to immolate myself in the hopes he will change his mind."

"Poor *Zanmi*," Alán murmured, giving Étienne a hug he did not realize he needed and Étienne sank into it, absorbing as much comfort as Alán would allow. Étienne had a wellspring of physical affection for Rafi and nowhere to expend it. Alán pulled back and studied Étienne. "Now what?"

Étienne laughed, the sound bitter and sharp. "Nothing. There will be a bachelor party, a rehearsal dinner, the wedding itself…" An endless parade of torturous moments in which Étienne would have to pretend Rafi had never meant anything to him. They would appear as everyone believed them to be— precarious allies with the singular goal of making the people they loved happy on the most momentous day of their lives—while inside, Étienne would die a thousand deaths. "We will send the bride and groom to their happily-ever-after and return to our respective lives."

"So sad," Alán said.

"It was good between us." Étienne got to his feet, picking up his camera and absently adjusted the lens. "But people break up all the time." He scraped his beard with his nails.

"Does not make your breakup any easier," Alán said.

"No, it doesn't." And ending things with Rafi was particularly bitter because it felt like a rejection of him as a person. He had been so sure they could build something more permanent together. But if he wasn't what Rafi wanted, then there was no hope of them having anything more than an affair, and Étienne's feelings had evolved too far beyond those boundaries. He wanted all of Rafi, or nothing at all.

He clapped his hands together, as if sending his morose thoughts scurrying into the dark. "It's time for a change."

Alán frowned. "I'm afraid to ask."

Étienne thought of the project he'd long wanted to work on in Jacmel—the one he'd discussed many times with his uncle, who still lived in the town— before the business of being Philip's best man got in the way. A photo series highlighting the beauty of Haiti, the resilience of his people despite the endless natural and historical tragedies. "It's not official but I'm considering a sabbatical after the wedding to do some work to benefit my city. A passion project and there seems to be no better time to do it."

Alán frowned. "You mean, you're leaving? What about your parents?"

"I will return to see them. It's time."

"Because of Rafi."

"Not just because of Rafi."

"But mostly because of Rafi."

"Alán."

"Zanmi." Alán draped an arm over Étienne's shoulders. "Don't you think that's a little extreme? To leave everything because of a broken heart?"

"A broken heart is the most compelling reason to make a change."

"But what will I do if you are gone? They will make me work with the LaRoux woman." He dropped his voice, a shiver washing through him. "She is a terrible, vulgar devil!"

Étienne snorted, and it was the first time he'd laughed in since things had ended with Rafi. "If you have tolerated me in this period, then surely, you can endure her."

"No-no-no." Alán wagged a finger at Étienne. "You are nothing like that remorseless misanthrope." He shivered again. "I will have to light a candle every day to ask forgiveness for all the terrible things I will think of her. I have half a mind to go find this Rafael and have a word with him. He's going to ruin my life!"

"You concern for me is truly heartwarming."

Alán examined himself in the mirror, smoothing out the fine black and orange striped cashmere sweater, the high waist of his slim black pans. "Of course I care about you. But your agony is contributing to mine. I don't see why you can't talk to him."

"No." The finality of the word echoed through the workspace. "I know my worth. I have had to fight too hard for everything I want—the respect of my family, a place in this country, even against Mother Nature herself." Etienne shook his head. He would not relent on this. "I have had to fight for my dignity. I won't compromise with my heart." Étienne's breath came to him in pants, but he took a deep breath, steadying himself. "I deserve to have someone love me with their whole chest."

Étienne set his camera on the table and hauled on his coat. "If I can't have that, then I would rather be alone."

"Étienne," Alán called, but he was already on the move, marching out into the hallway, avoiding the elevator in favor of the stairs. He'd taken a risk with Rafi and it had failed. This was his new reality. He'd experienced heartbreak before. But this one hurt him the most because it was the closest he had ever come to getting everything he wanted in a person.

Kat je kontre, manti kaba. The words Étienne had heard since he was a child came to him as he walked into the hotel he'd chosen with Rafi for the bachelor party. This event was one of many where they would have to put on a brave face and pretend they had been nothing but associates. Compatriots. In a generous retelling, perhaps even friends.

Face-to-face, we meet, no lies.

For Étienne, at least, it would be one, endless deceit.

Contrary to Rafi's original accusation at Val's engagement party, Étienne did have a strategy. He'd taken over the task of photographing the events of this evening from Alán in the hopes of occupying himself and placing a barrier between himself and the other groomsmen. One groomsman in particular, insulating himself so he could endure this night.

The hotel had been an excellent idea if Étienne could allow himself one moment of satisfaction. Cocktails had been set up in the lounge, where Philip stood, surrounded by a group that included three of his groomsmen—two cousins and a schoolmate Étienne also knew. Rafi was conspicuously absent, and Étienne quelled the impulse to message him and ask where he was. That was out of the question. He would not allow himself to do that anymore.

A pianist played instrumental music he had chosen from Philip's playlist, an odd mixture of movie scores, classical music and bad 90s-era pop.

"You have terrible taste in music," Étienne quipped when Philip greeted him, all his skills at dissimulation called to the fore.

Philip's cheeks, already flushed with the beginnings of the night's revelry, grew pinker. "Val's okay with it. That's what matters."

"You are not supposed to be thinking of your

bride-to-be this evening. You are poised on the precipice of matrimony, preparing to cast your life of singlehood behind you." Étienne threw his hand out with dramatic flair, while inside, each word was a thumb press, digging into an open wound. "These are your last moments as a man, alone against the world."

"Stop thinking of Val? That's not possible." Philip squeezed Étienne's shoulder. "You'll understand when it happens to you."

Étienne's smile faltered. "Hand me one of those cocktails, will you?" His voice shook and he tried again. "Just because you are the man of honor, does not mean you can monopolize the alcohol."

"Says who?" Philip pointed at the hotel foyer. "Everyone's here now."

Étienne schooled his face, anticipating the pain when he saw Rafi again, like an uppercut to his ribs. But this is what he did best. Pretend things didn't hurt. He'd had a lifetime of moving through spaces not meant for him, carving them out with wit, humor and, a few times, even brute force. What chance did a broken heart stand against a lifetime of that?

"Rafi," Étienne said, setting his face in stone, taking care that none of the wide-open fault lines in his heart appeared in his eyes. "We were waiting for you to begin the festivities."

Rafi froze, looking like someone had stunned him with a blinding spotlight. "I was…double-checking the arrangements."

"I did that last night," Étienne said. But how would he have known—apart from the occasional wedding-related text, it had been weeks since they'd spoken face-to-face.

Philip placed an arm over Rafi's shoulders, the third shot of bourbon making him expansive and oblivious to the tension between the two men. "A toast to your collaboration. I know whatever you guys have planned tonight, we're going to enjoy it." Philip clinked Rafi's and Étienne's glasses in turn. "Thank you both."

Rafi's face was pale against his open-collar maroon dress shirt, which was paired with snug black pants. Clueless and terrified and gorgeously, painfully irresistible.

Rafi needed time, he'd said. Time to think, time to react, time to know in his heart what Étienne had realized from the first moment they'd kissed but hadn't allowed himself to acknowledge. Étienne would give it to him. An eternity if he needed it. Étienne would just have to figure out a way to get through it.

Rafi clinked Étienne's glass, murmuring whatever banality he was expected to deliver in turn. He didn't look at him, his eyes fixed on some point beyond Étienne. With a grimace, Étienne hid behind his camera, adjusted the lens and said, "Say cheese."

Chapter Twenty-Four

Étienne

The night did not improve. Outwardly, the party was as entertaining as they'd intended, with intervals of feasting and drinking punctuated by the unique spots they visited—a churrasco dinner with live music featuring an endless parade of meats and tapas, perfect for absorbing the alcohol from the whiskey tasting that came after, followed by a late-night comedy club and a last stop at a *Star Wars*-themed sports bar with a private room playing a game televised earlier in the day that they'd all committed to ignoring in real time. Places and events Rafi had researched with the same painstaking diligence he did everything else.

But Rafi had danced around Étienne the whole night, his favorite avoidance tactic culminating in him sitting alone in a red, leather love seat, an open bottle of rum before him.

"Is he okay?" Philip asked about Rafi as he swayed at Étienne's elbow.

"He's just tired," Étienne lied. He'd been taking endless photographs, putting on the laughter and the small talk that descended into incomprehension as everyone except him got drunk off their gourds.

They returned to the hotel at an obnoxious hour of the early morning, a scratch before dawn. Étienne was certain they'd broken a few laws about being served alcohol on a Sunday morning, but he didn't worry about it as he herded everyone up to their rooms. Rafi, who he knew rarely drank, was slumped at the hotel bar, which had long been wiped down and closed.

"I think you've had enough," Étienne said as Rafi leaned heavily on his hand.

"A truckload wouldn't have been enough to get through tonight." Rafi hiccupped, his eyes fluttering closed. His gorgeous shirt was spotted with droplets of drink and his hair was wildly disheveled.

Étienne took a deep breath, slinging the camera over his shoulder and across his back. "Come on. Off to bed with you."

Rafi's bleary eyes opened as Étienne eased him off the barstool. "Promise?"

Étienne bit back a retort. What was the use? Rafi was so far gone, he'd probably fall asleep and forget everything when he woke. "Elevator is over there."

"You…hate…elevators," Rafi whisper-slurred.

"They are not my favorite but unless you'd like me to sling you over my shoulder, this is our only option."

"You've done it before," Rafi chuckled, leaning heavily against him. "I knew I shouldn't have asked the waitress to leave the bottle of rum. I was just too fucking miserable to resist it."

Rafi never cursed, and the shock surged though him like electricity. Étienne focused on balancing Rafi against his side, gritting his teeth as they entered the elevator. Rafi wasn't too incapacitated to walk on his own, but he did have a swerve in his step and, given his past difficulties with gravity, could have resulted in him landing on the ground again.

Rafi in his arms again was sending Étienne to a place of nostalgia and longing he didn't want to go.

"I'm sorry you have to be in here because of me," Rafi said, tilting his head up to look at Étienne.

"I'll be fine." Étienne focused on his hatred of this space, the automatic pounding of his heart, the evaporation of air. Maybe it was the elevator, maybe it was Rafi, but the feeling clawing inside his chest was exactly the same.

"I think Philip had fun."

"Yes," Étienne said, gritting out the word.

"You're the perfect best man," Rafi murmured as they moved through the elevator doors on their floor. "The whole time, I was just a backup… I got so heavily invested… Nobody asked me to…care so much."

Étienne, unable to make sense of Rafi's words, carefully searched Rafi's pockets until he found the magnetic card for the hotel-room door. Rafi yelped in surprise.

"What are you looking for in there?" Rafi leaned against him.

Étienne slid the card over the reader, the lock sliding open. "Here we go."

The room was shrouded in darkness. Étienne switched on a lamp. One arm still latched around Rafi, he flipped the bedding down and eased him onto the sheets. Rafi's arms sprawled out wide as if he'd lost control of them.

"I got so invested because of you."

"Because of your sister." Étienne's heart was ready to burst. "You should get some sleep."

"Because of you," Rafi insisted, eyes clear as glass. "Because I liked being with you. I miss... talking to you."

"Talking?" Étienne couldn't help himself.

"Hmmm," Rafi hummed playfully, waving a floppy wrist that quickly collapsed again. "Well, naked time was fun, too. But mostly," he sighed, and Étienne was sure he'd lost him to sleep before he whispered again, "I miss you." He slapped a hand against his stomach, aiming perhaps at his heart and missing dismally. "Your absence...it hurts right here."

Étienne shook his head to clear the foolish spasm of hope that erupted. These were the ramblings of a drunk man, not a declaration of devotion by someone fully committed to being with Étienne. Étienne did not want this, and surely, neither did Rafi. It was probably best that Rafi would forget everything because it would be impossible for someone as emotionally reserved as he was to get over what he had said tonight.

Sighing at his bad luck, Étienne pulled Rafi's shoes off, carefully undid his belt and eased his pants down. Rafi gave a small snort that was more like an arrested snore, a sound Étienne had never heard him make. He pulled a bottle of water from the refrigerator and placed it with a plastic cup and the magnetic room card on the end table before pulling the blankets over him. Rafi snored again, a loud and frankly obnoxious sound that made Étienne want to kiss him. He settled for thumbing the smooth space between his eyebrows before pulling away.

Rafi had clung to his need for thinking and logic over his affection for Étienne and hadn't tried to reach out to him once since Étienne had left. That said more than anything he could say when he was drunk. Étienne took one last look at Rafi, adjusted the curtains to keep out the morning light and left the room.

Chapter Twenty-Five

Rafi

Rafi woke to a ringing sound that lanced through his head like he'd been struck by the edge of the kitchen cabinet. He raised himself onto one elbow, careful about making any sudden moves, and searched for the source of the excruciating sound. The hotel-phone light blinking in time with the noise announced itself as the culprit and Rafi swore as he nearly knocked it over in an attempt to answer it.

"Good afternoon." It was Philip's inhumanely cheerful voice. "Everybody's waiting for you."

Rafi groaned. How had he overslept his alarm? Until he realized his phone was in his pants and his pants were… Who knew where his pants were? In fact, a quick glance under the duvet revealed that he was only in his boxers, having completely lost the thread of where he was and what purpose he was serving, the throbbing of his skull taking precedence over everything else. "Sorry. Give me fifteen."

"Take your time. Everybody's in the pool."

Rafi hung up and his head, which weighed a ton, only got heavier when the events of the night before rushed back to him.

A shockingly explicit string of curse words fell from his lips, in multiple languages, all conveying the same horrifying mortification at how he had allowed himself to gorge on rum until Étienne had had to drag him up to his room, after which he exposed his misery to him in the most embarrassing way possible before blacking out completely. At least, he hadn't puked on him.

Rafi didn't *think* he'd hurled his intestines all over Étienne.

It wasn't the sentiment that offended him—he missed Étienne, like he would miss oxygen, like he'd miss an arm or a leg, or the math part of his brain, which was actually the majority of his brain if he was honest. He'd blurted out of his feelings under the most humiliating circumstances, without any chance of mitigating the damage he'd done.

Rafi had to find Étienne and apologize. He owed him that much.

He made a cup of the anemic hotel-room coffee, doubling the dose with the hope that the shot of caffeine would make him feel human again. He showered and dressed before hurrying down to the pool area to find everything set up.

Rafi wasn't needed. Étienne was the best man and so far had managed all their plans like an orchestra conductor. Rafi's stomach burned with the memory of how he'd treated Étienne at the beginning—like an incompetent, when he was anything but. Étienne had been right about Rafi—he was judgmental and rigid and completely intolerable.

The buffet featured all the items they'd discussed, a perfect balance of breakfast and light lunch items that would go easy on stomachs made queasy by too much drink. The large-screen TV featured the Series-A soccer game everyone was watching. Groomsmen floated in the pool while outside the glass dome, buildings soared high around them. The sun shined, turning the globe into a ball that could barely contain the totality of Rafi's unhappiness.

Rafi searched the room, his eyes landing on Philip, whose attention was fixed on the screen. Rafi closed the space, waving at the grooms as he passed. "Where's Étienne?"

Philip turned, his hair and clothes impeccable, as if he hadn't jumped on top of the bar counter, wielding a light saber while shouting "For the republic! For democracy!" only a few hours ago. "He took care of the accounts and left."

Rafi couldn't imagine Étienne not staying with him to the end of the festivities. Had Rafi ruined this day for him, too?

"Was it work-related?" Rafi pressed.

"More like family. There's nothing left for any of us to do but eat, watch the game and check out."

"He's a good friend, isn't he?"

"The best, and I'm not saying that because I'm still a little drunk. He is one of the best people I've ever known."

Had it been anyone else, Philip's words could have easily been hyperbole, but when it came to Étienne, no exaggeration was too much.

Philip clapped him on the shoulder. "Hey, I appreciate you both. You guys did a great job."

But Rafi hadn't done a good job. Not by a long shot. Rafi had ruined this moment between Étienne and Philip. He'd ruined what might have been a good thing between them.

If you let me leave, I won't return.

The nausea that bloomed in his stomach had nothing to do with his hangover.

Philip was called away by a server, leaving Rafi with the weight of what he'd wrought. He hadn't deserved Étienne, in the end. Rafi possessed nothing that could tie someone like Étienne to him permanently. He was good, and decent and honorable and wonderful, and in the end, too much for Rafi to hold on to.

The effect of the hangover wore off after a few days. The effects of Étienne's absence did not. Val's text while he was at work made everything worse.

Étienne's coming over tonight to show us pictures from the bachelor party for our albums. Did you take any with your cell phone that you can send me?

The ache that pulsed through Rafi forced him to sit down. Étienne would be in East Ward, only a few blocks away from him. And Rafi had no right to see him, not after everything.

When I get off, I'll send them. What time do you need them by?

He'll be here at seven, so take your time.

Rafi stared at his desk, which was piled high with quiz papers and homework he no longer intended to grade for now. His mind wasn't working the way it should and he couldn't bring it back online.

When he returned home from work, he found his father at the entrance of Navarro's, placidly watching the people traffic. Rafi waved at him, trying to slip by him. His father stopped his escape.

"Have you recovered from the bachelor party?"

"Still feeling it," Rafi answered.

"Ah, to be young and willing to poison myself again."

Rafi gave an involuntary chuckle, but it sounded flat, even to his own ears.

Papi stepped aside, inviting Rafi inside the restaurant, then locked the door behind him. He waved at Rafi to follow him, which he did, taking the path he could walk with his eyes closed, from the kitchen of Navarro's through the door that took them to the building's main corridor and up to his father's apartment. Rafi took off his winter wear, removed his shoes, as was their family's shared habit, and entered the warm, cozy space of his father's kitchen, where a pot simmered over a low fire on the stove.

"Nati is always working and Val will be a married woman soon. It's just you and me and this *sancocho*."

Rafi breathed in the aroma of the traditional Puerto Rican chicken-and-vegetable stew. Hefty wedges of corn on the cob, chunks of green bananas, potatoes, carrots and chicken thigh floated in a bowl his father handed him, garnished with a smattering of cilantro.

"This was always the popular cure for a hangover. My mother would have it waiting for me, together with *un regaño* for exaggerating the night before. Even with a tongue-lashing from my mother, the *sancocho* made everything better."

Rafi gave him a small smile, the familiar spices soothing the melancholy that had taken up permanent residence in his heart. He stirred the soup with the spoon his father provided, blowing on it to cool it down.

"There are some things sancocho can't cure, *verdad, hijo*?"

Rafi shrugged, still stirring his soup. He always fussed at his students about shrugging, but he was starting to understand how there were some feelings that were too big to verbalize.

"Eat, *mijo*. Food tastes better when it's hot."

Hot things should be hot and cold things should be cold. Wasn't that what he'd told Étienne? Rafi was nothing more than a parrot, mimicking the most superficial of his father's lessons.

Rafi's heart picked up speed. He needed more than an inherited truth about hot soup. He was in a bleak mood, full of regrets he wasn't sure how to bury.

Papi took the chair across from him. *"Adonde está Étienne?"*

Rafi glanced at his father, who was staring back at him with a look that meant he wasn't in the mood for trifles.

Rafi closed his eyes, and for a moment, just felt the unhappiness flow through him and take root, like a bad roommate who refused to vacate. When he opened his eyes, he felt exposed. "He's at Val's."

"And why aren't you there, too?"

Rafi gave a bitter laugh. "Because I ruined everything."

"So? Fix it."

Rafi dropped his spoon on to the table, all the self-revulsion rising up to strangle him. "Didn't you hear what I said? I ruined everything. I don't deserve…" He tried to bite the words back but they wouldn't stay down. "I don't deserve him."

"That's not true."

"Papi, *perdoname* if I think your opinion is a little biased."

"Because I'm your father? Maybe my opinion is more valid because I know you better than anyone else. Do you know who you are?"

"You don't want me to answer that."

"That's okay. I will tell you. You are a good person, but you are a Navarro down to your last cell. You take too much on and you are too hard on yourself, and it never occurs to you that others might see you and value you for the things you refuse to see in yourself. *Y no es justo, mi hijo.* It's not fair that you hold yourself back from so much because of a misplaced sense of guilt."

Not this again.

"If you're going to tell me it's not my fault Mami's not here, I'm going to get up and leave."

Papi ignored that. "Then what is my excuse? I could have gone up to the school instead of letting your mother go. Is it my fault she's not here?"

"No!" Rafi retorted, horrified.

"And that boy who was teasing you? He could have minded his own business instead of being *un homophobico ignorante*, but he didn't. Was it his fault?"

It had never in a million years occurred to Rafi to blame the boy who had insulted him to the point that Rafi had hit him, prompting the principal to call his mother and ask her to come up to the school. "That's absurd."

"As absurd as you blaming yourself for something that was out of your control?"

"Papi, it's not the same thing."

Papi leaned forward. "She was supposed to be in the restaurant. If you hadn't gotten into that fight, your mother would not have left Navarro's to go get you. She wouldn't have gotten hit by that motorcycle and she would still be alive today. Tell me it's not what you think."

Rafi crossed his arms, his eyes beginning to sting. "You don't understand how something like that can make you feel."

"Can't I? Well let me tell you. You feel small. Insignificant. How could anyone ever want you, right? You question the love people send your way because it has to be a mistake, right? They don't know who they are giving their love to because if they did, they would keep it to themselves. They would stay away from you because how can someone love a man who took his wife away from her land to be buried in foreign soil?"

Rafi's was crushed by his father's words. "What? No, you can't think that way."

"And you can't think the way you do, because it's wrong."

Rafi brushed at the tears that gathered on his lashes. "Papi—"

"*Papi* nothing. It took me more than ten years to understand that no one is responsible for your mother, my *wife*, not being here anymore. Not me, and certainly not you. *Es la vida.* Life has no loyalty to anyone, so you must live it without remorse."

"I'm not like you." These words were starting to become a refrain.

"Look at me, *hijo*," he commanded and Rafi did as he was told. "Fix this in your mind so you don't waste any more time on useless guilt." Papi poked Rafi on the side of the head as he spoke with gentle insistence. "Bad things happen and you can't always predict or avoid them. But that doesn't mean you shouldn't fight to have every good thing that the life has to offer. Everything. Peace. Acceptance. Family. And the love of a person who is devoted to you. No one deserves it more."

Rafi took a deep breath, his heart pulsing and quaking and close to shredding itself apart. "How do I know that something bad won't happen and it will all end?" He didn't say *The way it did with Mami?* Or what he really meant—*What if I lose him?*

"You keep betting that something bad will happen, but there is just as much of a chance that good things are waiting. Why are you cheating yourself out of the chance to try?"

"I hurt him."

"Then you should be over there, fixing things."

"But…"

"You're scared." Papi leaned back. "If you lack courage, don't worry. It will come when you need it. But you both deserve a chance to be happy."

Rafi was desperately, completely in love with Étienne. Losing him at some point in the imaginary future would be terrible. But not having him at all was an outcome he could no longer live with, even if he couldn't see how things would turn out.

"Your sister made cheesecake for tomorrow's menu. She said if we touched it, she was going to give us a *paliza* with the broom."

Rafi snuffled into his sleeve. He'd have to wash the sweater, drenched as it was with his crying. "She's possessive of her desserts."

Papi's eyes twinkled in mischief. "I think, under the circumstances, even she would agree that this is a good reason to defile it."

"Defile it?" Rafi laughed through the last of his tears.

His father took his hand, squeezed it. "It's one of the few English words I like."

Rafi stood, leaving his soup unfinished, but he suspected his father wasn't going to call him out on it. "It'll have to wait. I have something to take care of first."

His smile this time was mischievous. "It will taste better if you and Étienne enjoy her dessert together, *si*? I think she will forgive you this time."

Rafi felt tears well again and he bit them back, tired of feeling this miserable. "Gracias, Papi."

Papi shrugged, but the pleasure he took at Rafi's words was evident in his shy smile. "*Vete*. You've made him wait long enough."

Rafi gave his dad a loud, wet kiss on his cheek before bolting out of his father's apartment, the heat of the spring day dissipating, turning the night air brisk. When he cleared the stairs, he paused for a few moments to text Val.

Is Étienne still there with you?

Her answer was instantaneous. He just got here.

Keep him there. And don't tell him I'm coming.

What are you up to?

Rafi skidded to a halt, his fingers tapping with a speed he didn't think himself capable. Help your brother out for once, will you?

Okay, but I expect all the details.

Rafi didn't even have time to be annoyed with her. He raced down the sidewalk in the direction of the waterfront. Philip and Val's apartment was a ten-minute sprint, and Rafi intended on cutting that time in half.

Chapter Twenty-Six

Étienne

Étienne printed drafts of the photographs he'd made of the bachelor party himself, making sure each one received the best technical treatment possible. The work had been a double-edged sword, requiring his intense concentration, the kind that could carry him away for hours.

But it had also wounded him because Rafi seemed to be everywhere. Each time his face appeared, whether posed or spontaneous, was another prick of a blade's edge, until the misery he'd been trying unsuccessfully to suppress bubbled up and overwhelmed him. He had been forced to step away several times, coming close to calling Alán to take over but he could not relinquish the task. Any chance to see Rafi's face was one he could not deny himself, even if it shred him to pieces.

He counted off the remaining stages of his commitment as best man, waiting with dread and hope as his liberation neared. The only things left were the rehearsal dinner and the wedding. The itinerary that would take him to his post-Rafi life, where he would strike out into the world and try again, this time leaving a part of his heart behind.

He drove to the flat Philip shared with Val, a beautiful condominium on the top floor of the complex Wagner Developments was slowly bringing to life—a benefit of being the heir of his father's company. Philip took the surrounding community into account as he developed his project, much of that a result of his relationship with Val. Étienne could appreciated this. He would turn his own life inside out if it meant sharing the rest of it with Rafi.

He gritted his teeth as he took the elevator to the top floor.

"You brought them!" Val clapped as she let him in. She looked stunning in a black-and-silver jumpsuit with a cashmere bolero sweater worn over the sequined bodice. The space was surrounded by glass overlooking the river and the skyline, as if Étienne could reach out and touch it.

Étienne tried not to stare at Val's face, tried not to tease out her resemblance to her brother.

"I keep my promises." He fell into the habit of his gregariousness. "Especially to you, Val."

Philip clasped Étienne to him in a warm hug.

"Thank you so much for this. You and Alán have been real life-savers."

"Can I offer you something?" Val took his jacket from him.

"Philip knows what I like. I'll arrange the photos on the table. They are yours to keep, regardless of which you choose to include in your album."

Philip went to the liquor cabinet while Étienne made his way to the desk in Philip's home office. Val quickly cleared space for Étienne to spread out his photographs.

A glass of scotch appeared in Étienne's hand as Val and Philip perused the selections. Étienne discreetly withdrew to give them privacy as he toured their apartment, all warm woods and clear spaces, bright interior accent walls and cheerful colors. Val loved her photographs and had an entire wall of their apartment dedicated to both her and Philip's families. Étienne paused before it, pretending not to be searching for one particular face among the collection. He found Rafi's graduation portrait, a smiling young man gazing into the camera bedecked in a blue graduation gown. His skin was soft, radiant with youth, and it was remarkable how much the Rafi of now resembled that young man, and all the subtle ways he'd changed since. Other photos, some at the beach, some around town, featured a few of the players Étienne had met at the basketball game. Rafi, in every iteration of himself except for the one way only Étienne knew, the one he would never forget.

"Hey."

Étienne turned at Philip's voice. Étienne's smile

was automatic. He'd always known how to project happiness, and never reveal his feelings when he was not.

"Frater. Do you like your photographs?"

Philip scrutinized Étienne. "Val is still looking through them." Philip came to stand next to him, scanning the pictures. His clear, blue gaze fell on the graduation photograph of Rafi that Étienne had been examining earlier. "I've always thought he was handsome."

"Indeed," Étienne agreed. "Difficult but handsome."

"He looked particularly handsome in the pictures you took of him. The *many* pictures you took of him."

Étienne groaned internally. He hadn't stopped to consider what the photos he'd showed them might appear to Philip and Val, having occupied a strange emotional place when he was sorting them, half-present, half-wishing he'd been anywhere but in his studio, alone, surrounded by the fractals of Rafi's face repeated over and over. He opened his mouth and closed it again.

"Are you going to be okay?" Philip put a gentle hand on his shoulder. "That's all that matters to me."

Étienne found himself in a dangerous place. He could pretend, but he could never fool Philip. It was one of the reasons he loved him. Philip was one of the few people who really saw him.

He scoffed in response, glancing into his scotch tumbler. "You know me. I am a hard tree to fell."

Philip tilted the contents of his glass into Étienne's. "Think you need this more than I do."

Étienne's chuckle was bitter but grateful. He clinked his glass against Philip's empty one and downed the whole thing in one gulp, the burn a relief. The sharp sound of a door buzzer cut through the apartment, and Val's quick, "It's open," came in response, putting Philip on alert.

"I'll go check it out. You know where the scotch is."

"I'm driving, I'm afraid."

"Lucky your friend always has a guestroom waiting for you." Philip winked before leaving.

Étienne sighed, making his way to the bar, where a bottle of aged scotch sat out. He refilled it and downed the shot without tasting it. He hadn't overindulged at the bachelor party—Étienne rarely got drunk as a rule, hating the way it made him feel the next day. But he was deep in his melancholy tonight and had nowhere else to be. He permitted himself to indulge another shot.

Étienne sensed someone's approach. He turned to see Rafi standing in the room, Val quietly disappearing as she shut the door behind her. The floor seemed to scroll away from Étienne and he had to rest the tips of his fingers on the table to ground himself. Rafi tossed his jacket onto a love seat, revealing the look Étienne had come to associate with his work—snug gray slacks, patterned dress shirt and a vest in the color family he seemed to favor, the color of spilled red wine. His hair, unruly on a good day, looked like a million fingers had run through it.

He looked heaven-sent and Étienne's body mourned him.

"Val told me you were here."

Étienne nodded. It explained his presence.

"You helped me the other night. At the bachelor party."

Étienne looked down at his fingertips against the wood, the only thing keeping him upright. "If you came all this way to thank me, please don't. I'm the best man. It's my job to manage the groomsmen."

"I know it's your job and you've always done it so well. I behaved as if you couldn't, but the truth is, you never needed me."

"What you saw was the result of our extensive planning. And that certainly involved you." Étienne eyes were still fixed on the wood of the table.

"Maybe. But my first impression kept me from seeing you for too long. I'm sorry for that."

"It was the same for me." *But only at the beginning.*

"Étienne, look at me."

Étienne forced his eyes from the table and his agony increased by orders of magnitude. "Happy now?"

"No. Not since you left."

"Rafi," Étienne pleaded.

"What I said the night you helped me to my room was all true. Those weren't drunk words. I confessed a truth I was trying to deny myself. I miss you. I miss us. I miss what we can be, and I'm sorry I ruined it."

Étienne heard Rafi's words, heard the string of sounds that made up each syllable, but didn't dare draw a conclusion because it would hurt too much to be wrong.

"What are you saying?"

Rafi stepped closer and Étienne's body felt like it was vibrating into the air. "I've always been ruled by fear, by a sense of shame and guilt that has poisoned so many things for me. But you didn't deserve…" Rafi raised a hand to touch Étienne and visibly pulled it back, thinking better of it. "You didn't deserve to have your heart broken."

"I…" Étienne, who never had trouble speaking, had difficulties finding words. "I shouldn't have rushed you. It felt like one rejection too many."

"I did feel rushed. Doesn't mean I couldn't have handled it differently." Rafi looked down at his hands, then looked up. "One thing being with you has taught me is that life is too short to not reach out with both hands and take the things that are meant for me. And you are meant for me. You're…how did you say? *Ou pafé*?"

"Please," Étienne said, unable to pretend. "Don't trifle with me. Mean what you're saying or don't say it at all."

Rafi took a ragged breath. "Sometimes I don't understand how someone like you can be with someone like me."

"Rafael…"

"No, it's okay. I'm working on not thinking that way." Rafi took a deep breath, as if shoring himself up. "I know I hurt you and I know I'm asking you to take another risk, but please." He reached out to place his hand over Étienne's heart, echoing another time Étienne had done the same. "I love you. We deserve this chance to be together."

Étienne waited for it all to disappear, for him to wake up and discover he'd been in a scotch-induced dream. He placed a hand over Rafi's, a shield of hands over his heart. Étienne reached with his other hand to slide his fingers up Rafi's neck, pulling him close so their layered hands were trapped between their bodies, their lips an exhale from each other's. Étienne paused, searching Rafi's eyes for any hint of hesitation, and finding none, said, "Kiss me."

Rafi relinquished himself to Étienne's command, closing the space between them. And when their lips met, it was sweeter than Étienne remembered. This was Rafi, without barriers or defenses, his favorite version of him, and Étienne tasted the surrender in his kiss, felt it in the way Rafi clung to him as if Étienne was the anchor that was keeping him afloat.

When they broke off, they held each other for a long moment until a shuffle came from beyond the door. Étienne gave Rafi a quizzical look as he pulled away and took his hand, leading him in search of the source of the noise. Opening the door, they found Val, clasped in Philip's arms, dabbing at her tear-smudged mascara.

"Are you okay?" Rafi asked.

"Yes. That—that was the most beautiful thing I've ever heard." She released Philip to pull both Étienne and Rafi into a group hug. "I knew you two would be perfect or each other."

"Va-a-a-al!" Rafi groaned.

Étienne glanced at Philip's face, but found it serene, even approving. "It's okay. She's just overjoyed for you guys."

"You're not…"

Philip's face morphed in surprise. "What? No, I want you to be happy. And if Rafi makes you happy, then I'm on board one hundred percent."

"Captain and skipper," Rafi murmured, and Étienne laughed, reveling in how good it felt. "There is something called privacy, *hermana*."

Val waved it off. "Oh, please. You should know better than that." She beamed at them. "I almost want to throw a party to celebrate!"

Étienne and Rafi glanced at each other before Rafi answered, "That'll be a big negative from us."

"Val, honey, maybe we should give them some alone time," Philip said.

"If you guys don't mind." Rafi scooped up his jacket. "We'll get out of here."

"I don't think I can drive," Étienne said apologetically. He was drunk on scotch and love.

"You won't have to." Rafi gave his sister a hug and a kiss, provoking a squeal of delight from her, before doing the same to Philip, who was clearly unaccustomed to the physical aspect of the Navarros' style of showing affection. "I love you both."

Philip flushed, obviously not used to that, either. Val answered for him. "We love you, too." She pulled Étienne in for another surprisingly strong hug before Rafi hustled them out of the apartment.

Hooking his arm through Étienne's, Rafi steered him toward Navarro's.

"Are you taking me home?" Étienne asked, eager to get Rafi alone and show him how much he'd missed him.

Rafi stopped, the streetlamp casting shadows that played and danced against the pavement. He placed a hand against Étienne's cheek, the warmth of his palm seeping down to his heart. "My place. Papi has a whole cheesecake for you. He said, when I was done making up with you, he would have it waiting for us."

"Enrique?" Étienne was dizzy with everything that had happened tonight and, again, he was out of words.

"Or didn't you know? My family's already claimed you for our own. You get me, and you also get a bonus order of the Navarros."

Rafi kept leaving Étienne's speechless, and in response, pulled him in for a kiss that meant other kisses were close behind, each one belonging to Rafi. Rafi hadn't stolen all his words, though.

"I love you, *cheri*. So much." And the smile Rafi gave him was incandescent with joy, transforming his face, making him young with expectation and bright with the promise of the many days that awaited them. Endless days framed in changing lights and colors and seasons. Days they would no longer spend alone.

Epilogue

One year later

"Best summer vacation ever."

Étienne, who was reclining on the double-wide chaise lounge they shared, lifted his gaze from his paperback, prescription sunglasses covering his face. Rafi, for his part, was trying not to doze off and burn under the afternoon sun. As if he'd been born to lie on the private beach of a million-dollar, beachfront villa in Dorado, Puerto Rico.

"And whose idea was it to come here?"

Rafi groaned, covering his face with his *pavo*, or straw hat. "I forget who I'm talking to."

Chuckling, Étienne leaned over and pulled Rafi's hat from his face. Rafi began to protest but Étienne descended on him, lips pressing against lips, tongue slipping into his mouth with licks of wet fire. Rafi's mind bleached to white like the sand surrounding them. When Étienne pulled back, his face hovered over his, glee rendering it brighter than the azure sky that sprawled like a cape behind him before it vanished into the aquamarine sea. "My ego requires constant maintenance."

Rafi was giddy with a glittering rush of love that made him grateful he was lying down, or else he'd fall on his face again. "I thought you were joking when you said you had permission to come to this estate whenever it was available, but I was wrong."

The book slid between them as Étienne propped his head on his arm to better look down at Rafi. "The owner and I have been friends for many years. She has always offered me the use of her home when she is traveling on business, but I never had a reason to do so."

"Until now?"

"Until you."

This time, it was Rafi who pulled him down for a kiss, the sensuous tempo of the sea matching the tightening of desire low in his belly. It spread through his limbs, his chest, his heart. Rafi was never going to get used to the easy way Étienne expressed his love for him. But with time and patience, he was learning to be easy, as well.

It had been more than a year since Val and Philip's wedding and each moment had been like this. Hot and sweet and full of surrender. All that fear of chaos and disorder had come to nothing, though there were times where compromises and recalibrations had to be made. But they always found a way to meet somewhere in the middle.

Rafi's life was so much richer because of it. He loved Étienne's family, who kept referring to him as Profi no matter how many times Étienne corrected them. Rafi especially adored Jo-Jo and Jacq, who awoke in Rafi a desire for children of his own, a desire he clutched tightly to himself like a secret treasure. For now.

The rush of terror at how close they'd come to not having any of this still made Rafi stop and catch his breath. Rafi wanted more of this. He wanted it forever.

Tension twisted his insides, not for the reasons that used to scare him—once Rafi had dropped his defenses against Étienne, he never put them up again. He was nervous because he was going to do something the Rafi of only the year before would've never dreamed of doing. The Rafi before Étienne had come into his life and made him brave.

"Let's order in," Rafi said as they tidied their lounge area.

Étienne dumped their towels in a bamboo basket inside the patio. "No dancing on Atlantic Beach tonight?"

Rafi curled his fingers between Étienne's, pulling him toward their suite…and the Jacuzzi waiting for them on the balcony. "I have other plans tonight."

Later, Rafi set out clothes alongside Étienne's. The day they landed in San Juan, they drove directly to a clothing store Olivia's mother and Rafi's aunt recommended in the old city. There, they picked up several, short- and long-sleeved, linen guayaberas in cream, ecru, powder-blue, yellow and white, each shirt woven through with shimmering threads of blue or deep green. They bought matching linen shorts, slacks, leather sandals and the *pava* hats Rafi wore everywhere. Étienne was a vision in those bright colors, sleeves folded to his elbows, the contrast striking against his deep brown skin, while powerful thighs shifted beneath the material of his pants, and his perfect square, pale nails against brown toes poked through the leather of his sandals.

Rafi had learned a critical detail about Étienne— his love of beautiful things also included clothes. He sought out well-made, expensive pieces, which he cared for the way collectors preserved vintage cars. It was the only area in which Étienne reached Rafi's level of meticulousness. For everything else, Étienne lived in a natural state of entropy. The number of times Rafi stumbled over used towels and haphazardly tossed papers was a testament to this fact.

Dinner was *rellenos de camarones*, grilled red snapper, and a fresh conch salad topped with parsley and drizzled in lemon and oil brought from a well-reviewed restaurant that was two miles past the artery leading to Puerto Rico Highway 2, which ran from east to west, parallel to the coastline. Rafi was nervous as he cleaned up, but if Étienne suspected he was up to something, he showed remarkable restraint in not asking about it.

"I want to show you something," Rafi said.

The stars over the Atlantic were breathtakingly

bright as they walked westward along the shore. Rafi had done his research—after the collapse of the Arecibo Observatory in 2020, visits to its observational platform were out of the question. But there were other things to see, things that Étienne, with his sensitivity to visual stimuli, would appreciate. The moon was new, the absence of light rendering the pinpoints of stars in the sky more visible.

"It's hard to see, but that cloudy patch right there is the center of the Milky Way. I'm told it can be seen clearly from the bioluminescent bay in Guánica. You'd love it."

Étienne lifted his face in the direction Rafi pointed. "When we were young, we hiked in the mountains north of Jacmel. There, the Milky Way is a ribbon of diamond and pearls across the sky."

Rafi smiled at the image. "I booked a tour of the bay. It's not a long drive and we can visit my aunt and her family on the way back. You can take all the pictures you want."

"I like this plan. Thank you." Étienne beamed. Unlike Rafi, he loved to meet new people, deriving energy from the thrill of new situations. Rafi was the complete opposite and was content to let him take the lead. In ways both large and small, Rafi had learned to hand the reins over to Étienne.

"We just make sense, you know?" Rafi blurted out. Étienne raised an eyebrow and Rafi cursed his inability to say beautiful things like Étienne could.

"When I was single, I thought I could rationalize my way toward finding someone to love. I even made a list."

Étienne's eyes caught the light of the stars, and sparkled. "Let me guess—a spreadsheet?"

"Will you tease me forever if I say yes?"

"Most definitely."

The burst of air Rafi released was part nerves, part laughter. "Yes, I made a spreadsheet. And if I had tried to match you to the requirements I outlined, you would have failed."

Étienne's laugh broke into the air like a song. "You know how to seduce a man."

Rafi took both of Étienne's hands in his, growing serious. "You failed those requirements and I thank god every day you did. Because whatever the hell I wrote in those cells would never have made me as happy as you do."

Rafi pulled a hand away. Étienne tracked Rafi's every movement as he pulled a small box out of his pocket, black velvet imprinted with gold lettering from a jeweler Dariel recommended, one who understood exactly what Rafi needed. Étienne went still, his face draining of all flippancy, his mask of good humor and charm falling away.

"Once, I accused you of going too fast and here I am, doing the same thing. I can slow down. I can wait twenty years or we can do this tomorrow. With or without ceremony. It doesn't matter." Rafi thought of Papi's words, that he would always find the courage to do the right thing when he needed it, and this was the most right thing he would ever do.

Rafi opened the box, two simple gold bands resting in the velvet interior. "I want to spend my life with you, and we can do this any way you want. You have all the control, as long as whatever we do ends up with you and me being together."

Étienne smiled and it was pure and simple and entirely his. "Yes."

"Yes?" Rafi wanted to slump in relief. "Because if it's too sudden, or you have some other arrangement in mind…"

"You're overthinking again." Étienne lifted his hand, his thumb tracing its familiar path that started between Rafi's eyebrows, smoothed over his forehead and down his cheek until Étienne held his chin in his hand. "I somehow knew from our first kiss that you were the man of my life. I had no idea how it would happen, or even *if* it would happen, but I knew." His eyes flickered toward the star-bedecked sky. "It's not too soon, and it's not too slow. The timing is perfect. *Ou pafé.*"

Trembling, Rafi fixed Étienne's ring onto the finger of his right hand, and watched the same tremor overtake Étienne when he placed the other on Rafi's. Hands clasped, fingers tangled, they held them pinned between their bodies as they fell into a kiss that was a promise of forever, the sand and sea and gauzy center of the Milky Way their witnesses. And everything truly was perfect.

* * * * *

#2971 FORTUNE'S FATHERHOOD DARE
The Fortunes of Texas: Hitting the Jackpot • by Makenna Lee

When bartender Damon Fortune Maloney boasts that he can handle any kid, single mom Sari Keeling dares him to watch her two rambunctious boys for just one day. It's game on, but Damon soon discovers that parenthood is tougher than he thought—and so is resisting Sari.

#2972 HER MAN OF HONOR
Love, Unveiled • by Teri Wilson

Bridal-advice columnist and jilted bride Everly England couldn't have predicted the feelings a sympathetic kiss from her best friend would ignite in her. Henry Aston knows the glamorous city girl is terrified romance will ruin their friendship. But this stand-in groom plans to win her "I do" after all!

#2973 MEETING HIS SECRET DAUGHTER
Forever, Texas • by Marie Ferrarella

When nurse Riley Robertson brought engineer Matt O'Brien to Forever to meet the daughter he never knew he had, she was only planning to help Matt see that he can be the father his little girl needs. But could the charming new dad be the man Riley didn't know she needed? And are the three ready to become a forever family?

#2974 THE RANCHER'S BABY
Aspen Creek Bachelors • by Kathy Douglass

Suddenly named guardian of a baby girl, rancher Isaac Montgomery gamely steps up for daddy duty, with the help of new neighbor Savannah Rogers. Sparks fly, but Savannah's reserved even as their feelings heat up. Are Isaac and his baby too painful a reminder of her heartbreaking loss? Or do they hold the key to healing?

#2975 ALL'S FAIR IN LOVE AND WINE
Love in the Valley • by Michele Dunaway

Unexpectedly back in town, Jack Clayton is acting as if he never crushed Sierra James's teenage heart. When he offers to buy her family's vineyard, the former navy lieutenant knows Jack is turning on the charm, but no way is she planning to melt for him again. But will denying what she still feels for Jack prove to be a victory she can savor?

#2976 NO RINGS ATTACHED
Once Upon a Wedding • by Mona Shroff

Fleeing her own nuptials wasn't part of wedding planner Sangeeta Parikh's plan. Neither was stumbling into chef Sonny Pandya's arms and becoming an internet sensation! So why not fake a relationship so Sangeeta can save face and her job, and to get Sonny much-needed exposure for his restaurant? It's a good plan for two commitmentphobes...until their fake commitment starts to feel all too real.

Get 4 FREE REWARDS!

We'll send you 2 FREE Books plus 2 FREE Mystery Gifts.

FREE Value Over **$20**

Both the **Harlequin® Special Edition** and **Harlequin® Heartwarming™** series feature compelling novels filled with stories of love and strength where the bonds of friendship, family and community unite.

YES! Please send me 2 FREE novels from the Harlequin Special Edition or Harlequin Heartwarming series and my 2 FREE gifts (gifts are worth about $10 retail). After receiving them, if I don't wish to receive any more books, I can return the shipping statement marked "cancel." If I don't cancel, I will receive 6 brand-new Harlequin Special Edition books every month and be billed just $5.49 each in the U.S. or $6.24 each in Canada, a savings of at least 12% off the cover price, or 4 brand-new Harlequin Heartwarming Larger-Print books every month and be billed just $6.24 each in the U.S. or $6.74 each in Canada, a savings of at least 19% off the cover price. It's quite a bargain! Shipping and handling is just 50¢ per book in the U.S. and $1.25 per book in Canada.* I understand that accepting the 2 free books and gifts places me under no obligation to buy anything. I can always return a shipment and cancel at any time by calling the number below. The free books and gifts are mine to keep no matter what I decide.

Choose one: ☐ **Harlequin Special Edition**
(235/335 HDN GRJV)

☐ **Harlequin Heartwarming Larger-Print**
(161/361 HDN GRJV)

Name (please print)

Address   Apt. #

City   State/Province   Zip/Postal Code

Email: Please check this box ☐ if you would like to receive newsletters and promotional emails from Harlequin Enterprises ULC and its affiliates. You can unsubscribe anytime.

Mail to the **Harlequin Reader Service:**
IN U.S.A.: P.O. Box 1341, Buffalo, NY 14240-8531
IN CANADA: P.O. Box 603, Fort Erie, Ontario L2A 5X3

Want to try 2 free books from another series! Call 1-800-873-8635 or visit www.ReaderService.com.

HARLEQUIN PLUS

Try the best multimedia subscription service for romance readers like you!

Read, Watch and Play.

Experience the easiest way to get the romance content you crave.

Start your **FREE TRIAL** at
www.harlequinplus.com/freetrial.